I0666652

BEYOND THE SHADOWS

THE FORCE OF NATURE SERIES

AMBER LYNN NATUSCH

Beyond the Shadows - Force of Nature Book Three
© 2017 Amber Lynn Natusch

ISBN-13: 978-0-9970765-9-2

Beyond the Shadows is a work of fiction. Names, characters, places, and incidents either are the products of the author's imagination or are used fictitiously. Any resemblance to actual persons, living or dead, businesses, companies, events, or locales is entirely coincidental.

Published by Amber Lynn Natusch
Cover by Regina Wamba, at Mae I Design
Ebook Formatting by Pure Textuality PR
Editing by Kristy Bronner

http://amberlynnnatusch.com

ALSO BY AMBER LYNN NATUSCH

BEYOND THE SHADOWS

BENEATH THE DUST

The *ZODIAC CURSE:*

HAREM OF SHADOWS Series

EVE OF ETERNAL NIGHT

Contemporary Romance

UNDERTOW

More Including Release Dates

http://amberlynnnatusch.com

www.facebook.com/AmberLynnNatusch

http://www.subscribepage.com/AmberLynnNatusch

For my mother,
because she's everything.

ACKNOWLEDGMENTS

As with any book, it took the help of many people to help reach the final product. I have to thank Shannon Morton, Kristen Bronner, Courtney DeLollis, Madeline Sheehan, Jena Gregoire, Kristi Massaro, my husband, Bryan, and my amazing fans. Without you all, the success of this series never would have happened.

PROLOGUE

"We need to talk," he said, stepping back from me. The distance between us made my chest hurt more than it ever had. I couldn't stand being apart from him. "You and I—we have a common interest. A mutual enemy."

"Who?" I asked, my voice thin and wavering.

He cocked his head at me, curiosity in his eyes. "The fey queen."

He took another step back from me, and I felt my body lurch forward, reaching for him.

"I will kill her," I replied. I sounded wild and feral, ready to shred her body to bits just to have him all to myself. He laughed at my response, the warm tenor of his voice caressing me in places it should not have.

"It won't be that easy," he said, coming closer. "But I will give you something in return. Something you desire."

"You?" I asked, reaching for his face.

"Peace," he said, stroking my cheek. "You do know that you cannot have them both, don't you? They will never concede to that." He circled behind me, his fingertips dancing along my jaw and down my neck. My breath caught in my throat, the trail of burning they left in their wake an exquisite torture. "But what if there were another option?" he mused, stopping behind me. "One that could give you everything they had to offer without the sacrifice? Without the pain and indecision you clearly suffer from?" He pressed closer to me, his chest grazing my back, his lips at my ear. "What if there were a door number three?" His whispers sent chills up my spine. "I wonder, Piper... do you like pain? Is that why you are unwilling to let them go?" He traced the lobe of my ear with his nose. "I could give you pain..."

Just as my body began to sink into his, I felt it jerked away like a dog on a leash. I struggled against the force, already missing his touch. I looked back at him for aid, but he simply smiled.

"I will send for you soon, Piper. Tell Knox I said hello..."

Then he disappeared.

Grizz shot me a dubious look as I laced up my sneakers. He seemed perplexed by what we were about to do, as though he'd forgotten how we met in the first place back in Alaska. It seemed like so long ago in that moment.

"For the third and final time, it's called running. You literally just go out and run for an indeterminate amount of time, then stop. It's for exercise," I explained, shooting his fluffy rear end a scathing look. "Something you could use, by the look of it."

He drew his head back as though offended by my words, then promptly walked around me, poking me in the ass with his muzzle as he circled back. He sat down with a thud in front of the door, looking rather pleased with himself. My reaction only furthered that self-satisfaction. He practically beamed with pride as I started to stammer out my response.

"Are... are you kidding me? You think *my* ass is getting fat? I'm not the one laying around letting Kat hand-feed me all day long." He snorted and looked away as though unimpressed with my argument. "You listen up, furball. You will go running with me right now and you will like it. I can't have you getting killed because your tubby butt is slowing you down." Grizz snorted, but I cut him off with my index finger in his face. "Remember, Drake gave you your man suit, but I can get it taken away if you start shirking your responsibilities. You'll be stuck back here at casa de vampire... is that what you want?" His low growl was answer enough. "Good. Now let's go."

He moved aside so I could reach the panel by the door, and I punched in the updated twelve-digit code. We'd tightened up security since the fey queen had somehow breached the wards on the property and attacked us. Knox, Drake, and Merc had spent days afterward crafting newer, better ways to keep her from doing it again. I didn't want to tell them that I thought their efforts were in vain. They seemed to need the peace of mind that doing something gave them. Men were fixers; who was I to take that away?

I opened the door to the safety breezeway that led outside as Kat came down the stairs, looking like she'd had a wild night. Her short auburn hair was tousled and there were dark circles under her eyes. Somehow she made it all look good, but it was uncharacteristic to say the least. Either she hadn't slept or she'd been on a bender—maybe both.

"You hardly look like you're up for this, but I'll ask anyway. Wanna go for a run?"

She yawned as she ran her hand through her hair.

"Hard pass on that, my friend. I need food. And coffee. Then more food."

"Rough night?"

She let out a humorless laugh. "You could say that."

"I didn't hear you come in."

"Because I only came in an hour ago."

I looked down at my phone. It was 1:37 p.m.

"Sooo..." I started, trying to figure out how best to broach the subject. If Kat was imploding because we no longer had immediate danger pressing down upon us, I needed to figure out how to shut that down without her realizing it. "What did you get into last night? An entire fifth of JD?"

"'Fraid not, Piper. Though that sounds good right about now. Maybe I'll put some in the coffee." She flashed me a grin as she passed, headed for the kitchen.

"For the record, day drinking alone is called alcoholism!" I called out after her. She gave me a thumbs-up over her shoulder and kept moving toward the kitchen, never breaking her stride. I looked over at Grizz, who watched as she disappeared around the corner. He turned concerned eyes to me. "I know, buddy. She's still struggling with Jensen's death. Kat needs distraction. If she doesn't have one, she'll make one. I'm going to need you to stay close to her, okay?" He nodded once, an awkward bob of his massive head. "Good boy. Now let's go slim down that rump of yours."

GRIZZ and I must have run the property for about an hour before my legs grew shaky and unstable. I stopped a few feet past the tree line and bent forward, holding myself up with my hands on my knees. The bear who'd packed on a few pounds put me to shame in the running department, and the smug look on his face said as much as he looked back at me and strutted toward the mansion.

That was officially the last time I'd ever comment on his husky shape.

"Wait up!" I called, jogging over to him. It took more

effort than I would have admitted, but I had to at least try to save face. I'd been feeling off ever since the fey queen had attacked us at the mansion and I'd torn a hole in the veil to save Jagger. I'd inadvertently restored Drake's amulet in the process, but I wondered at what cost. I looked down at the pale blue marking on my chest and sighed.

Yet another problem to solve.

Like a good little guardian, Grizz stopped to let me catch up. Just as I reached his side, one of the many black SUVs owned by the vampire enforcers came tearing into the driveway, appearing through the magical wards in a flash. One second, there was nothing; the next, dust and gravel flew as the hulking vehicle skidded to a stop by the front door.

Foust and Brunton jumped out of the front seats and ran around to the back. Not a good sign. Grizz and I sprinted to meet them. Jagger climbed out of the back seat, practically running into me.

"What's going on?" I asked, panic in my voice. He grabbed my hand and led me to the back of the SUV, where I found a gory sight. Benji, one of the youngest wolves in the pack (both in human and werewolf years), was mangled so badly I barely recognized him. Without a word, I put my hands on the worst of the injuries I could see and called forth my magic to heal him. I closed my eyes, expecting the usual blinding white light to come, but it was slow and faint, nothing like it had been only days earlier. I tried to tamp down my rising panic and focus on healing Benji—not worry about the implications of my weakened magic.

When the warmth of power slowly washed away, I glanced down to find Benji looking rough but uninjured. Foust put his hand on my shoulder and gave a squeeze—a silent thank you for saving his lupine brother. Brunton hauled Benji out of the back and helped him walk into the mansion, shooting me a nod over his shoulder.

"Do I get to know what just happened?" I asked, turning to Foust for answers.

"Honestly? I don't have a fucking clue. One second, we were getting out of the SUV to get groceries. The next, we heard Benji scream and found him lying beside it, bleeding to death. Brunton threw him back in the car and we bolted. Jagger held pressure on the worst of the wounds until we could get him back here."

"Where was Knox?" I asked.

Foust and Jagger shared a look before speaking. It was only then that I saw how covered in blood the ginger-haired wolf was. Caked in it might have been a better description.

"Trying to find Mack," Jagger said, the embarrassment in his tone plain. He still blamed himself for the ambush that had almost resulted in both him and me being captured by the fey queen. It hadn't really been his fault, but he didn't see it that way. Even after receiving the pack's forgiveness, the poor guy hadn't forgiven himself.

"Did you call him?"

"We couldn't reach him," Foust said. "I left a message and a text. Either way, though, he should have felt the attack on Benji. He'll know someone was hurt and follow that feeling back here."

"Except he's fine now," I pointed out.

"True, but he'll come anyway. It's impossible for him not to."

As if on cue, another black vehicle—one of the sports cars in the fleet—came flying into the driveway, grinding to a halt next to the SUV. Knox practically jumped over the top of the low car to get to us.

"Who was it?" he asked, running toward us.

"Benji," Foust replied. "But he's okay. He's inside with Brunton. Piper fixed him."

Knox let out a loud exhale—a sigh of relief—then grilled Foust and Jagger on what had happened. Once he was caught up, he raked his hand through his hair, his tell that he was trying to calm himself down. The hint of gold flaring in his eyes faded away, leaving only crystal blue in its wake. I loved those eyes so much. I hated seeing the pain in them.

"He'll be fine, Knox. They got him here in time."

"Foust drove like a fucking maniac," Jagger said, trying to help.

"Good," Knox replied, heading toward the entrance. "I'm going to go check on him." He stopped in front of me, wrapping his arms around my neck to pull me against him. He wound his hands in my hair and massaged my scalp, then kissed the top of my head. "Thank you, Piper."

"You know I love the boys. I'd do anything for them."

He pushed me away to look down at me, a proud but sad smile stretching across his face.

"I know you would," he said softly. "That fact only makes me love you more—and scares the shit out of me at the same time."

I let out a little laugh and followed Knox as he led the way inside, Grizz and the boys behind me. I was glad the boys had gotten Benji back in time and that I had been there to help. But the whole ordeal illustrated a problem that I had no idea how to avoid in the future. If the war around us was growing more widespread and vicious, how could I possibly keep all of them safe—especially with powers that had seemed to be on the fritz ever since I faced off against the fey queen? The wolves? The enforcers? All those who had come to my aid when I'd needed it? There were so many of them and only one of me. Sure, Jase, Dean, or Merc could ghost me around, taking me somewhere in a flash if need be, but they were limited to the cover of night. The wolves were not. They could find trouble at any hour of the day—at any place in town.

And I couldn't always be with them.

2

Benji sat on the massive sectional in the media room, chowing down on a plate full of food. Kat and Brunton were with him, trying to get him to answer questions between mouthfuls. When it became apparent that it was going to take way too long that way, Kat stole the plate from his lap and put it down out of reach. Benji, refueling after his attack, growled at her, his animal side edging out the rational one. Kat quirked a brow at him and stood, ready for whatever he planned to do. Brunton, however, wasn't having any of it. He shot to his feet and towered over Benji, cowing his aggression in that single move. When Brunton appeared satisfied that the kid had gotten the message, he backed away, letting Benji have a little breathing room.

"So like I was saying," Kat said, as though there hadn't almost been a fight, "what do you remember seeing?"

Benji let out a breath and flopped back against the plush sofa. He closed his eyes as though he were trying to replay the event in his mind. He winced at some point, and a surge of anger shot through me. Whoever had attacked him had wanted to kill him.

"I didn't see anything," he said, frustration in his tone. "I jumped out of the back seat and went to shut the door. The next thing I remember after that was blinding pain and collapsing to the ground. I never heard anyone approach. Didn't see the attacker. If I didn't know better, I'd think it was a ghost."

"Did you smell anything?" Knox asked, walking around the couch to sit by the young wolf.

Again he closed his eyes and focused on the attack.

"Maybe," he said. "But I can't describe it. It was a strange smell—like nothing I've ever smelled before." He dropped his gaze to his lap. "Sorry I'm not more help, Knox."

"It's okay, Benji," the alpha replied, looping his arm around the wolf's shoulders. "I'm just glad you're okay. We'll find who did this. I promise."

Brunton shot Knox a dubious look. Apparently he was less confident the culprit would be caught.

"What about the rest of you? Did you smell anything weird?" Knox asked. The three of them all said the same thing—no.

"What now?" I asked, not thrilled to know that some crazed supernatural was running around.

"For now, we proceed with caution until we know more about this assassin."

"Assassin?" Foust repeated.

"What Benji described was a hit for sure. Quick. Clean. No evidence left behind."

Foust grunted in agreement.

"Why Benji, though? He has no history with this place. Hell, he's from the opposite side of the country."

"I'm aware of that," Knox replied, his tone a bit more

biting than necessary. "But if we can figure out the why, we might be able to figure out the who."

"Unless it was a totally random act carried out by some psycho," Kat pointed out unhelpfully. "There's a war going on. There's a lot of power up for grabs. It's hardly like any of the breeds wouldn't ally themselves with someone like the person who did this just to get ahead."

"She's right," Brunton agreed. "Until he strikes again, we can't draw any conclusions."

"So we just let this killer run loose in New York City until he attacks us again?" I asked, thinking that was a shit plan if ever I'd heard one.

"You want to go on the offensive?" Kat asked, mischief in her eyes.

"Maybe..." I started, cutting myself off so my mind could catch up with my mouth. "Maybe I can track him down. I found Drake, right? Maybe I can find this guy."

"You had something to connect you to Drake," Knox pointed out, his voice kind but firm. "We don't know anything about this guy."

"Or girl," Kat added.

Knox nodded in concession. "Or girl."

"I still think it's worth a try," I said, formulating a plan. "But we should wait until Merc, Jase, and Dean can go too. Their ghosting abilities could come in handy with this."

Knox's lips pressed to a thin line. "Agreed."

"Well, looks like we have some daylight to kill until then," Kat said, grabbing Benji's plate of food from the coffee table. "If you need me, I'll be fueling up for a fight." With fork in hand, she sashayed out of the room, shooting Brunton a sharp look as she passed him. Whether it was a thank you for his earlier help or a warning to stay the fuck out of her business, I couldn't tell. But I could tell that

Brunton found it wildly amusing. His devilish smile told me as much.

"She's right," Knox said, getting up from the couch. "We need to get ready. Whatever or whoever attacked Benji got the drop on him. We can't afford for that to happen again." Knox looked down at Benji and offered a sad smile. "You're going to have to stay home for this one, Benj. I know Piper fixed you up, but I'd feel better if you held down the fort."

Benji nodded, the sign of a good little submissive wolf, then stood up and walked out of the room. I felt bad watching him leave, the slope of his shoulders saying all there was to say. He was embarrassed by what had happened. He felt like he couldn't hang with the rest of the boys, which wasn't true. It was no small feat to take down any werewolf. Whoever had done it in such a ninja-like way had to be beyond formidable. The fact that we were going to hunt it later made my stomach queasy.

How the hell could Kat and the boys eat at a time like that?

The room cleared out slowly, until only Knox and I were left. He looked at me from the other side of the couch, the concern in his eyes plain.

"It's bad, isn't it?" I asked, walking around the sofa to stand before him.

He nodded. "It's bad enough that this thing brought Benji down without him even defending himself, but he or she did it right under the noses of the other three. Benji's practically a pup, but Foust and Brunton? They're as old as I am. Their skill sets are honed. So how in the world did this thing do what it did without even being seen?"

"I don't know." I hesitated for a second, not really wanting to bring Merc's name up at that moment, but the truth was that he might have an idea who could have done it. "Maybe Merc would know?"

Knox's expression soured. "Possibly."

He walked past me and through the exit and stormed down the hallway, headed for Merc's room. I scrambled to catch up with him, worried that he'd say or do something to provoke Merc. Those two could get into it about almost anything, a truth that had been repeatedly illustrated in the days following the fey queen's attack. Virtually any mention of that night set the two of them off in epic fashion. The rest of us had learned not to bring it up, but it didn't seem to matter. They'd find a way to argue over the color of the sky if they were around each other long enough.

The strain of their relationship was starting to get to me.

Knox pounded on the bedroom door until Merc opened it, filling the doorway with his imposing frame. He stared at Knox like he wanted to remove his head from his body until he saw me at his side. His expression softened slightly, but its hard edges were still there. I felt my chest tighten in preparation for the showdown.

"One of my boys got attacked in broad daylight today while they were out. None of the guys saw anything. According to Foust, whoever did it nearly killed Benji. They got him home just in time for Piper to save him." Merc flashed a look of approval my way, then returned his attention to the alpha before him.

"I take it you've come to me with a plan, so tell me what it is."

"Once night falls, we're going hunting. And you and your brothers are coming with us."

"Do you have anything to go on, or should we just wander the city looking for something we cannot identify?"

Knox's shoulders bunched as his anger grew.

"Piper is going to see if she can use her magic to track it somehow."

Merc's eyes went wide at that comment.

"She is not a divining rod for trouble."

"Actually..." I started before his rather pointed gaze cut me off.

"Let me rephrase. You are not a magical tool to be exploited whenever the situation demands. You put yourself on the line to save Jagger and nearly found yourself a permanent captive of the queen." Though I understood where his anger came from, it still hurt to have it turned on me.

"Merc, I don't see any other options. We can't let whatever it is run free and you know it."

"I have no intention of letting this being run free, but I also have no intention of using you to track it. Surely the wolves can put their noses to good use and sniff it out."

His tone was condescending at best, and it was clear that Knox didn't appreciate it. At all.

"If you and your brothers want to stay home like a trio of pussies, go for it. The boys and I can go out and do your job for you if we have to."

"And Piper?" Merc asked, casting a wary eye down at me.

"She's a big girl. She can decide for herself what she wants to do."

Knox turned and walked away, his trail of anger lingering behind him in the hall. I couldn't blame him for that; Merc hadn't exactly been kind during their interaction. Knox had almost lost one of his wolves. A smidge of compassion wouldn't have killed Merc.

"Piper," Merc said, stepping out of his room to join me in the hall. His dominating presence seemed to crowd the vast space in a way it shouldn't have. "This plan—if one can even call it that—I think it's unwise."

"Maybe, but if you had seen Benji..." I cringed at the memory of the boy bathed in blood lying in the back of the Suburban. Merc put his hands on my shoulders and squeezed, pulling me back to the present.

"And I don't want that to be you. That is my point exactly."

"Give me a little credit, Merc."

"I do. A lot, in fact. But you have no idea what this being is. That lack of information alone makes this extremely dangerous."

"Then come with us! Get Jase and Dean, and let's go find this thing."

His mouth pressed to a thin line and he took a deep breath. He clearly didn't like the idea, but he knew I wasn't going to drop it. If I was going to do something he deemed reckless, he'd agree to go just for his peace of mind. That and to keep me safe. Somehow, after all that had happened in our time together—all he'd seen me do as my powers came to me—he still wanted to protect me, when in truth, the tides had turned. I was probably more capable of protecting him—at least when my magic wasn't glitchy.

I think that reality didn't sit well with him. For his sanity, I would have to let him think he could.

"So should I go hunt down those two clowns and let them know we're leaving at nightfall?" I wound my arms around his waist for a little extra persuasion.

At that, he laughed.

"Your tactics, though appreciated, are far from subtle, Piper."

"But are they working? That's the real question."

He feigned a serious expression. "Unfortunately, yes.

They are." He pulled away from me, turning to head down the hall to where his brothers' rooms were. "I shall alert Jase and Dean and fill them in on this weak plan of Knox's. Jase will have concerns. Dean, however, will be elated. He loves harebrained schemes like this."

"Hey!" I shouted in mock offense. "It's partly my harebrained scheme too, you know!"

He looked over his shoulder at me and flashed a dark smile.

"Of course it is. Never a dull moment with you, Piper Jones."

3

Merc had called his brothers' reactions to the plan with eerie accuracy. When we all finally assembled in the foyer, Jase's expression was full of uncertainty, whereas Dean couldn't have looked more pumped. He was raring to go. I thought he was going to scale the walls if we didn't let him out soon.

"What's with him?" I asked Merc, watching as Dean flipped a dagger over and over in his hand.

"He just ate," Merc replied, a hint of amusement in his voice as we took in the show.

"Oh..." Then I thought about his food options in the house. "Wait! Who'd he eat?"

Merc's eyes drifted across the room to where Kat leaned against the wall. She looked at me and shrugged.

"What can I say? The weirdo likes my blood."

I heard a low rumble echo through the space, the high ceiling allowing it to continue on for a while. I expected to find Grizz staring daggers at Dean, but when I located him in the crowd, he looked totally unfazed. Clearly not the source of objection in the room.

"We take four vehicles," Knox said, cutting off my train of thought. "Merc, you and your brothers can take a few of my boys. The rest of the pack that's going will split up among the other three."

"And Piper?" Merc asked, leaning closer to me. Knox did little to hide his contempt for the gesture.

"She's riding with me. If she needs a boost in power, I'll be there to give it to her."

"And if she needs it cut off?"

Here we go...

"Then I guess you'd better be nearby."

"I'll go with you. Foust can join my brothers."

The finality in his tone was plain. There would be no room for further discussion as far as he was concerned.

"Fine. Let's go," Knox replied, leading the way outside.

The group filed out: at least half of Knox's pack, Kat, Grizz, and the three brothers. The rest of the enforcers had made a point of being involved in other matters that evening. I felt the rift between them and the wolves grow a little wider that evening. I hoped it wasn't a trend that would continue.

"Shotgun!" Kat shouted, making her way toward one of the massive SUVs. Brunton, Jagger, and a handful of wolves packed into that vehicle, the rest piling into the others. Foust found himself riding in the passenger seat next to Jase, with an overenthusiastic Dean leaning against his seat. Foust shot me a desperate look as I passed by, and I couldn't help but laugh. The misery in his eyes helped calm my nerves a bit, distracting me from the mission we were on, if we were actually on one at all. That would rely on me entirely—on my ability to somehow connect to and pinpoint the assassin's location.

I climbed into the SUV with Merc and Knox, settling

into the passenger seat next to the alpha. Merc leaned against my seat as Dean had Foust's. Even in the simple matter of seating arrangements, he seemed to not want to be one-upped.

"Okay Piper," Knox said calmly. "See if we can get this tracking party started." He gave me a tight smile and reached over, putting his hand on mine.

I returned his expression, then closed my eyes, hoping that I hadn't oversold my ability—that I could find a way to use my magic to find him. While I focused, he started the car and backed out, rolling to a stop at the end of the driveway. I muttered under my breath, hoping that I chose my words well and the magic would understand what I wanted. It always had in the past.

That night proved no different.

"Find the one who attacked Benji," I said, waiting for whatever sign would lead us to him. A rush of wind came through the window I'd cracked, wrapping itself around me. Then it withdrew with such force that it pulled my hair through the narrow opening. Without thinking, I unhooked my seatbelt and bolted from the SUV. Merc was at my side in a second, silent as he surveyed the grounds.

The wind danced along the driveway, kicking up dust as it went. It painted the way toward the woods I'd run in that afternoon. For a moment, I wondered if the magic had misunderstood me somehow, but with every second I hesitated, the force of the gusts grew, nearly knocking me forward. I stumbled into Knox as he rounded the back of the vehicle. His questioning stare quickly turned to one of understanding.

"He's here."

The others started to climb out of their respective vehicles, wondering what in the hell was going on—if maybe our search was over before it started. But the moment the wolves took in Knox's expression, they knew otherwise. The collective growl they let out was evidence of that fact.

The group began to run, following the trail of dust and wind as it led toward the tree line. Merc and Knox flanked me, with Grizz at my rear. I felt a strange sense of déjà vu as we crossed the part of the property where the four of us had stood against the fey queen. It was then that I wondered if she was behind the whole thing—if whoever had attacked Benji was one of her fey assassins. Maybe she wanted to toy with us like the sadistic cat she was.

The wind grew stronger as we broke through the wall of brush and ferns. I felt it drawing us closer to the gorge and the bridge that crossed it. That made me nervous in and of itself. What a perfect place to level your enemies, dropping them hundreds of feet to their deaths. But the wind's path changed, leading us away from the bridge and certain death. Instead, it circled back toward the mansion. I stopped, breathing hard as I looked at how the leaves danced in its wake.

"Something's wrong," I said, my voice raspy.

"It's leading back to the house," Kat observed, sounding as irritated as I felt. "Are you sure we aren't just chasing our tails here?"

"No," I replied honestly. "I'm not."

Then a scream cut through the night air, raising every hair on my body. It was somewhere between human and wolf, and the group broke into a dead sprint toward the mansion the second we heard it. Knox and Merc led the charge, the others trailing right behind them. Unable to keep up with their pace, Grizz and I pulled up the rear. I asked the winds for a gentle push and soon found myself back in the chase. But when I arrived, I wished I hadn't.

I could hear Knox shouting as we neared, calling a name over and over again. There was an urgency to his voice, a fear that rocked me to my core. Pain. So much pain. When I pushed my way through the crowd, I found him kneeling on the ground with a limp body in his arms. I dropped beside him, hoping to help, but just as it had been with Jensen in Faerie, I was too late.

Benji was already dead.

4

"I told him to stay inside," Knox said, his anger belying his sadness. "What the fuck was he doing out here?"

"Knox," I said, gently pulling his arm away from the body. It was then that I saw the head had been completely severed. A wave of nausea rolled through me. "Knox... let's go inside. We need to see if anyone in there knows why he was out here."

I looked up at Foust and he nodded, bending down to take Benji's body from Knox. A tiny growl escaped the alpha as Foust reached for the dead wolf, and he backed off. I put my hand on Knox's face, pulling his attention to me.

"It's not your fault," I said softly. "We're going to find who did this..."

Brunton, who must have checked the perimeter of the mansion, ran into to the driveway, a look of concern in his eyes. Brunton never looked concerned.

"Knox," he said, doing his best to ignore Foust as he successfully took the body—and head—from Knox and walked away. "We need to talk."

"What?" the alpha roared, snapping his head to look at Brunton.

"Not here," he replied, jerking his head to the empty yard at his right.

"Just say it," Knox growled, rising to his feet.

"I caught a scent..."

Knox straightened at his words. "Who?"

Brunton shook his head. "Not a who—a *where*."

I looked up at Knox and found wide eyes staring at Brunton. "Show me."

The two of them took off in the direction Brunton had just come from. I followed along, Kat and Grizz at my side. I could hear Jase and Dean behind me, theorizing about what Brunton had found. Rounding the far side of the house, we nearly ran into the two wolves.

"Motherfucker," Knox said, slamming his fist into the brick exterior of the mansion. Dust and mortar clouded the air around us, and I coughed as it filled my lungs.

"What is it?" I choked out.

He didn't reply right away. Instead, he stared at something behind me, and I turned to follow his gaze. It landed on Merc.

"Faerie," Knox said, his stare never faltering.

"That fucking bitch!" I shouted, frustration and anger coursing through me.

"No." Knox's voice pulled me from my downward spiral. "Not the queen. The king."

Holy. Shit.

"But..."

"Perhaps he's come to reclaim what he views as his," Knox continued, ignoring my outburst. "Or maybe he's come to cut us all down one by one."

"You belong to the fey king?" Kat asked, her tone incredulous.

Knox nodded. "Technically you do too."

At that, she scoffed. "I don't belong to anyone. Let him try to take me. I'll make him wish he hadn't."

"Yeah?" Knox asked, taking a step toward her. "Just like Benji did? Is that what you want?"

"He could try," Kat replied, folding her arms across her chest.

"And he'd succeed. You have no idea what he's capable of..." Knox's words trailed off as he looked over at Brunton and Foust, who'd rejoined the group. The three of them shared an understanding that the rest of us didn't. I knew that the wolves had been created by the fey king. That he ruled them in his realm. But what we didn't know—or hadn't known before that moment—was whether he could control them on Earth. It seemed highly likely, given Benji's actions.

Something had compelled him walk out to his death that night.

"The fey king would not come here alone," Merc said, his deep voice cutting through the fear and tension in the crowd. "This is not his doing."

"I agree with the vampire," Brunton said, shooting a look of disdain at Merc. "The king didn't do this but he sure as fuck is behind it. Benji wouldn't have recognized the scent because he was never in the king's realm."

"But we were," Foust said, looking at Knox. "We are his originals."

Silence settled around us. Even the normal sounds of the night seemed to hush at Foust's admission. As if those words held weight with the world itself.

"He is sending a message," Merc said, breaking the eerie quiet.

Knox pinned his golden stare on the vampire and growled.

"Then I guess we'll be sending him one in return."

ONCE WE ENTERED THE MANSION, Knox grilled the wolves who had remained behind as to what had happened. Only one of them had seen Benji leave the media room, heading for the grand staircase that led to the foyer. He hadn't said where he was going, but upon further interrogation, we learned that he hadn't looked like himself. The wolf who'd seen him had chalked it up to everything that had occurred earlier that day; that he still must have been feeling low. Benji had never said a word.

Nobody had heard him slip out the door.

"It can't be a coincidence," Brunton said, looking at Knox, who nodded in agreement.

"He was compelled. I'd bet my life on it."

"Compelled by whom?" Kat asked, drawing out the 'm' far longer than necessary.

"The fey king."

"But the vamp over here says that nutjob wouldn't come here, so it can't have been him."

"I said he wouldn't come *alone*," Merc countered.

"I haven't worked out the how just yet," Knox replied, his irritation plain. "But he's behind it. I explicitly told Benji to stay behind—a *direct* order. If he disobeyed it, then something overrode my authority."

"Like the fey king," Brunton added.

"Could he have a surrogate of sorts?" Jase asked.

"Someone he could imbue with that ability to send in his stead?"

The trio of wolves shrugged.

"It's been so long," Foust replied. "I have no idea what he's capable of anymore."

"We left there for a reason," Brunton added. "He's a genuine psycho. I have no doubt that, if he wanted to, he could figure out how to puppet someone on this side of the veil to impose his will."

"Which is what?" I asked, still trying to piece everything together. "I mean, he wouldn't kill you if he wanted you back, right? So why kill Benji? That won't accomplish that goal."

"Perhaps he means to leverage me into returning," Knox said, his voice low and threatening. It sent a chill up my spine. "I will go if it keeps him from killing any more of my pack." I knew he meant what he said, and it scared me. If he thought it would save his boys, he would go to the fey king willingly.

Not a fate I was willing to accept.

"It won't come to that," I said, but my voice lacked the conviction it needed to sell my sentiment.

"You can track the surrogate," Jase said, placing a gentle hand on my shoulder. "We should try again."

"Sooner than later," Dean added.

"No time like the present," Kat said, punching in the code to the security door. "If that fucker wants to skulk around on the property, then let's flesh him out and show him just how much we appreciate his visit."

"And if he can compel you too?" Brunton asked, staring daggers at her across the foyer. "What then?"

She scowled at him, walking back through the doorway into the house.

"I haven't met a man yet that can compel me to do anything." Her words were jagged and dangerous, threatening to cut through Brunton just as the mystery attacker had cut through Benji. "I'll take my chances."

Before he could reply, she turned and walked through the door that Grizz held ajar for her, leading the way outside. I followed her, knowing the others would as well. There was safety in numbers—or so I hoped. I had a feeling nobody would be going out alone on the property until I had a chance to talk to Drake about the wards and blocking the trespass of the fey king or his minion.

We all huddled just outside the mansion, and I got right down to business.

"Take me to the one who killed Benji."

Nothing. Not a stir of wind, not the call of a bird. Absolutely nothing responded to my call. I tried three more times before the reason came to me. It was so obvious I was frustrated with myself for not realizing it sooner.

"He's gone back to Faerie," I said, turning to address everyone behind me. "I can't track him from here."

"So what? You just randomly keep calling for him until he's on this side of the veil to find?" Kat asked, sounding pissed.

"I don't see another way, short of going to Faerie after him."

"NO!" a chorus of voices shouted in unison. There were so many I wasn't even sure who all had chimed in, but their sentiment was clear. Nobody was going to the other side to hunt down the killer. Like it or not, we were the mice to his cat in his little game of chase.

"Okay. No Faerie. I got it," I replied, putting my hands up in surrender. "But we can't just do nothing. Let me talk to Drake, see if he can help us."

My eyes darted from Merc to Knox and back again, hoping that they could at least agree to that plan, and my suggestion would not bring about yet another fight. When neither said anything, I let out a breath, that damn spot in my chest loosening a notch.

"Call him," Knox finally said. "See if he can come over right away."

"You're certain he can be trusted?" Merc asked, his voice gentle but his accusation anything but. "He was the one who warded the property after the queen paid us a visit. Perhaps he is not entirely on our side."

"Merc, he came to our aid when we needed him most," I said, shocked that he hadn't accepted my mentor, especially after all he'd done. Yes, he was a cagey bastard, but so were most of the men in my life, so what was new about that? He'd shown me that when the chips were down, he'd be there, and that was good enough for me. "You don't need to trust him, but I do. And we need all the help we can get on this one. Drake was Reinhardt's number two. He knows things that we don't."

"I'm with Piper on this one," Knox said, folding his arms across his chest. "He helped save Jagger. He's good with me."

Merc's expression darkened, clearly unhappy to be in the minority on the issue.

"There is something about him I don't like," he said, his dark eyes narrowing. "His secrets run deeper than most." Merc made a point to shoot a glance at Knox after he spoke. The gesture wasn't lost on the alpha.

"If you've got something to say, then say it."

"I have made my opinion clear on the matter." He softened his expression when he looked down at me. "I just don't want you getting hurt."

"None of us does," Kat said. "But I don't want anyone

else getting fucked up either, so if we need the homeless magician to help us out, then I'm down with that idea too."

"Homeless magician?" a voice called from the darkness. The group all startled, turning to look down the darkened driveway where the voice had come from. Moments later, Drake appeared, a wicked smile on his face. He'd meant to sneak up on us, the crazy bastard.

He was so not helping to rebut Merc's argument.

"Kat has a way with words," I said, forcing a smile.

He cast her a sharp look. "Indeed she does."

"We need your help," I said, stepping apart from the group to meet my mentor. He walked down the gravel way, looking more disheveled than usual that night. Either he hadn't slept for days or he'd been in a fight—something along those lines—because he looked weary. It made me wonder what he'd been up to and where exactly he was living. When I'd first met him, he'd been in the basement of an abandoned building, living with human addicts and the homeless. In all that had happened from that point on, I'd never thought to ask whether that was actually his home or if he was just lying low, living under the radar while the war waged around him.

It also made me wonder where the rest of his kind were —our kind.

"I know," he said, surprising me. Seeing the shock written all over my expression, he explained. "I could feel your magic. You were working overtime to find something— or someone. Since I was nearby, I thought it best to check in on you and see what trouble has landed on your doorstep."

The group quickly filled him in on the events of the evening. By the time Drake was up to speed, a dark shadow covered his features, his expression ominous. Not a great sign.

"The fey king is not to be trifled with," Drake said, as though I hadn't figured that out already. "Nor are his creatures." For the second time that night, Knox was on the receiving end of a pointed look.

"I already know about that," I told Drake. "I know about the wolves." The warlock's eyebrows shot up in mock surprise.

"Well isn't that encouraging."

"Can you fix the wards?" Knox asked, ignoring Drake's jab. "He got to Benji right here. We can't have that happen again."

Drake looked thoughtful for a moment, then nodded.

"With the amulet intact, I should be able to."

"Good," Knox replied before taking a deep breath. "I'd appreciate it." He looked at the faces of the wolves around us, then turned back to Drake. "We all would."

Drake nodded once, his genuflected gaze drawn out longer than necessary.

"Now if that matter is settled," he said, looking again at me, "I'd like to speak to Piper. Alone."

Nobody moved.

"We'll be fine out here. The fey king's toy is gone. I'll be right here," I said, pointing to where my feet were planted in the gravel.

Still nobody moved.

I thought I was going to have to plead my case until Kat finally turned, holding her arms out wide to corral the men around her into the house.

"Okay boys... let's let the warlocks have a sidebar. We can go inside and eavesdrop from there." She looked over her shoulder at me and winked before pointing to the intercom by the front door. "This thing comes in super handy sometimes."

I shook my head in mock disbelief, then watched her practically shove the guys through the entrance. Some of them went without too much of a fight. Merc, however, was a different story. Even after Knox had disappeared into the breezeway, Merc remained, staring at Drake and me. The heaviness of his stare made my chest hurt, and not in a good way. Whatever suspicions he held against Drake, they were going to be a problem.

Kat gave up on him and walked in, shrugging back at me as if to apologize. But Grizz was having none of it. He walked up to the vampire, shoved his face into Merc's, and snarled—his way of telling him that guarding me was his job, not my mate's. The gesture was received about as well as could be expected, but to Merc's credit, he didn't touch the man-bear. Instead, he let loose an inhuman roar of his own before turning on a dime and storming into the house. I stood there wide-eyed for a moment, my heart racing. I'd heard a similar sound the night he'd tried to kill me. The memory echoed through my veins as my blood pounded through them.

The door closed behind Merc, and Grizz stood guard, giving me a nod to let me know he had the situation on lock. I choked on a laugh, realizing that where I was concerned, the bear was suicidal at best. It only made me love him more.

"So what's with the secrecy?" I asked, turning to face Drake. I found shrewd eyes looking right through me, like he'd found something inside of me that he didn't approve of.

"Something is weighing on you, Piper," he said, his brow furrowed with concern. "Something beyond the obvious threat of the fey king's lackey and the possibility of retribution from the queen."

"Thanks for that reminder," I said, scoffing at the mention of the queen. Yet another looming problem.

"My apologies," he said, stepping to the side with his arm out—an invitation to follow him away from the house. "But that is your reality. You cannot afford to deny it."

"I know that," I said softly, kicking at the gravel as I walked.

"Good. Now tell me what is bothering you."

I shook my head, letting out a loud exhale. "I'm just tired, Drake. I've been exhausted ever since the night the fey queen attacked us."

No longer sheltered by the shadows of the mansion, the bright light of the moon shining down on us, he looked me over, his eyes narrow and scrutinizing.

"You look unwell."

"Thanks," I replied with a laugh. "You really know how to make a girl feel better."

"Come here," he said, reaching his hand out to me. With hesitation, I went to him. He placed his hand on my forehead and closed his eyes. His expression tightened every now and again as though he heard something he didn't like. After a minute, he released me and opened his eyes.

A storm was brewing behind them.

"You don't feel right to me. Your magic... it's interrupted somehow."

"I know!" I shouted. I felt bad the second the words left my mouth, and I took a deep breath to calm myself before apologizing. "I'm sorry... I didn't mean to do that. I'm just... it's just that..."

"You're on edge?" he asked rhetorically. I nodded anyway. "Is there anything else you're not telling me?"

I considered his question for a moment until the aching in my chest grew to a level I couldn't ignore. I didn't want to tell him about the mark because I didn't want him to freak out like I knew the boys would if they found out. I didn't want someone telling me what to do or how to feel, but Drake's observation about my magic combined with my own concerns made me nervous.

"I need you to not freak out about this," I said, setting the ground rules before I showed him the fading mark on my chest. "If you can't do that, then I'm not telling you."

His mouth pressed to a thin line, clearly unhappy about my stipulation, but he eventually nodded in agreement. Satisfied that he would at least try not to wig out, I pulled my crew-neck tee down low enough for Drake to see the faint blue marking on my chest. His eyes went wide the second he saw it, his hand flying up to touch it.

"Why didn't you tell me about this?" he asked, sounding angry and terrified simultaneously.

"Because it was fading and I knew what it was from. It wasn't like I woke up with a blue spot on me and had no clue why it was there."

"But you have no clue what it's done—what it might have done," he replied, glaring at me for a moment before returning his gaze to the mark on my sternum.

"I've had a lot on my mind," I said softly, not wanting to get into that particular conversation.

"I'm sure you have." His acerbic tone was duly noted. Drake wasn't the biggest fan of my love life; as a general rule, he avoided the topic. I wondered if he was about to change that policy. "Piper, I must be honest with you. I fear healing the amulet may have affected your magic somehow."

"And I'm assuming not in a good way, right?"

His expression soured.

"I can't know that yet. You did say that the mark was

34

fading. Have you felt any better than you did right after the fey queen's attack?"

I considered that for a second, thinking it hadn't been that long ago. I'd barely had two seconds to myself in that time, between Knox and Merc and the drama going down in the city. Did I feel better? Maybe. But maybe not. I just couldn't tell.

"I'm not sure."

"I need you to monitor this closely for the next couple of days. If it improves, then it's likely you just needed to recharge from the energy you expended that night." He looked at me thoughtfully, backing up a step to give me some space. "You did rip a hole in the veil between here and Faerie, and fix the amulet."

"Not a bad day, huh?" I forced a smile at him that earned me one in return.

"Not bad at all—except that if you plan to go against whatever the fey king has sent for you, you will need to have all your abilities."

The wind in my sails died.

"What can I do?"

His lips pressed to a grim line, slashing through his even grimmer expression.

"I don't know yet, but I'm going to leave this with you," he said, drawing the amulet out from under his shirt. "You can have it once I shore up the wards against the fey king's magic. If you did in fact give a part of yourself to this, it should help balance you out until you heal."

"Okay," I replied, staring at the blue glow of the stone I'd healed the night the fey queen attacked. I expected the pain in my chest to ease when I took it from him, but it didn't change. My nerves shot through the roof. What if I really had given a piece of myself to the amulet—a piece I could never get back?

He took it from my hands and started off toward the dark edge of the property.

"I'll return in a minute," he said. "Stay with the bear until then. And don't worry, Piper. We'll figure this out."

Though I found some comfort in his conviction, there wasn't enough to pacify my concern. I walked back to Grizz, my worries plain on my face, and he opened his arms. He folded me into them, pulling me against him. It still felt strange to be close to him in man form, but there was never anything sexual about it. He was the same old Grizz, furry or otherwise. He just wanted to keep me safe.

And as I looked out into the darkness where Drake had disappeared, I wondered if he would have his work cut out for him.

5

When I came back into the mansion, I headed straight for my room. I collapsed onto the bed and pulled the blankets around me, not even bothering to undress. It was so late that it wouldn't be long before the sun was up, demanding I rise as well. All I wanted was a few hours to escape the reality of my life.

Apparently Grizz wanted the same.

Still in his human form, he flopped onto the bed next to me, launching me off the mattress for a second before I bounced back onto it. I let loose a tiny shriek, caught off guard by the motion. It wasn't surprising that I had been on the wrong end of that teeter-totter. What was surprising was the massive arm that flung across my chest and pulled me into a rock-hard body.

I lay there for a second, wondering if my assessment of our relationship had been wrong, but then I looked back at his face. His eyes were closed from exhaustion. A light snore escaped his mouth. Nope, he was still just Grizz. I tried to think about the bear behind the man and how we'd always snuggled up. It must be so hard for him to navigate his new life in NYC and his new form. Even though my body wanted to jump out of the bed and demand he sleep on the floor, I couldn't. He was my buddy—my Grizz. The bear that had saved me. Even if he looked like a rugged lumberjack with an attitude problem, he was still the same grizzly inside.

With that in mind, I took a deep breath and tried to relax under the weight of his arm.

It wasn't long before sleep pulled me in, but it wasn't peaceful at all. I was restless, unable to fall into her depths and stay there until the morning light dragged me out of her hold. Flashes of a dark enemy tormented my brain; whispers from an assassin who eluded me. Then, cutting through those images, Merc appeared, his form distant and faded but there nonetheless. I tried to pull him to the front of my mind, but it wouldn't cooperate, my sleep not deep enough to allow him in. His words intermingled with those of the fey king's killer, sounding like a poorly overlaid music track. My brain fought to separate the two, but it was useless.

Then Merc disappeared entirely, and I shot awake in bed. Grizz, still beside me, leapt off the bed and growled, his gaze shooting around the room for a danger that didn't exist. It took a minute before his shoulders relaxed and he looked down at me, confusion in his stare.

"Sorry Grizz. My fault! All my fault. There's nothing wrong, I just..." I cut myself off, not sure I wanted to go into an in-depth explanation of my tormented sleep. But it soon became clear that the man-bear wasn't going to let my abrupt wake-up slide, so I told him. Once I finished, he looked at me with concern and suspicion in his eyes. "It's fine, buddy. I just—I'm having a hard time with everything.

And I'm exhausted. I haven't slept well since we had to save Jagger, and now all this shit with Benji and the assassin..." My chest tightened and I mindlessly rubbed at it until I realized Grizz's eyes were fixed on the hand making circles along my sternum. I dropped my hand to my lap, but the damage was done. The silent interrogation began the second he quirked his eyebrow. "My chest hurts, that's all." His arms folded across his chest, the gesture looking a lot like a certain alpha werewolf we knew—not that I planned to point that out. "Fine! I told Drake about it tonight, and he thinks I drained my magic to heal the amulet and need to recharge or whatever. He's looking into it, so don't freak out, okay?" I took his utter lack of reaction to what I'd said as a no. "What do you want me to do, Grizz? We have to trust him. You do trust him, don't you?" Grizz nodded once, a barely noticeable movement of his head. But given their history, it was huge that he did in fact trust the warlock. The two of them hadn't exactly gotten off on the right foot. My guess was that Grizz's opinion had changed the minute Drake gifted him with a way off the property. That man suit of his had come in really handy. He had no intention of biting the hand that had provided him with it.

"Okay then," I said, climbing out of the bed. "That settles it. For now, we leave it to Drake to sort out the mystery behind my chest pain. Agreed?" Grizz gave me a dubious expression, but nodded. "Good. And no telling the others," I said, realizing just how stupid that sounded. Nobody else seemed to understand Grizz like I did, except for maybe Kat. I made a point to make sure he knew how fast I'd pull his man-suit privileges if he let her in on things, and he made a show of letting me know how much he appreciated me leveraging him into silence.

Whoever'd taught him how to flip me the bird was going to get a mouthful.

I made my way into the bathroom to get cleaned up for the day. It was then that I realized I'd gone to bed with blood on my hands and clothes. I made a mental note to strip the bed and burn the sheets. I wanted to get rid of any memory of that evening.

Thirty minutes later, I emerged to find a fluffier, snugglier Grizz sitting next to my bed. I gave his head a scratch as I walked by, grabbing some clothes off my dresser. I pulled up the jeans and threw on the tank before heading toward the door, pulling the off-the-shoulder sweatshirt on over it. It seemed colder in the mansion than usual.

Or maybe it was just me.

It was early yet, and I wondered if the wolves would be up and at 'em or still passed out in their various shared rooms. It had been a long night for everyone, but especially them. They'd lost one of their own, and that was a hit to them as a whole. I'd never seen how they honored their dead in Alaska. We'd never had the time. But I knew that Benji deserved to be put to rest, and I hoped that we'd have the opportunity that day to do it. The pack needed to. I could feel it in the stillness of the house.

I popped down the butler's stairs to the empty kitchen and grabbed some pastry off the counter. Grizz hovered by the box, nudging it with his nose before climbing up onto the counter and burying his head in it.

"I can come back for you later," I said with a laugh. "You look pretty into what you're doing there." He didn't even bother to come up for air at my snide remark. Instead, he kept on devouring Jagger's favorite snack. He was going to be so pissed when he saw that Grizz had eaten all of them. Especially since he was making such a mess of doing so.

I walked out of the kitchen, shaking my head as I took a big bite of the sugary, flaky goodness. With my mouth stuffed full, it made sense that I'd walk right into Merc. The amusement in his eyes was plain. Damn him and his inability to sleep when he should.

"You're up," I said, my words garbled by the food in my mouth. Little puffs of powdered sugar blew out as I spoke. I had the good form to look embarrassed, but he just smiled at me, no doubt finding my antics endearing.

"I can wait for you to finish that if you'd like." He leaned against the wall for good measure, crossing his arms over his chest.

"Actually, I'm not even that hungry." I walked back into the kitchen and tossed the danish across the room at the bear. It hit him in the head, and I took off before he could come after me. "So," I started, trying to be casual as I raced down the hall away from the angry grizzly in the kitchen. "What are you doing skulking around the house? Shouldn't you be sleeping or something?"

"I have business to attend to," he said, pushing off the wall to stand before me. The way he loomed over me made me wonder if that business had to do with me—more specifically, what was inside my pants.

"Oh... okay."

"I tried to come to you last night."

"So that did actually happen," I muttered under my breath. Of course he heard me just fine. He looked at me with intense curiosity.

"You saw me?" he asked, surprised. "You never replied."

"Sorry," I said absentmindedly. "It was weird... I was having a dream about the faceless killer—the fey king's pet —and I could hear him saying things to me, even though I don't think it was actually him. You appeared at some point, but it was different. You weren't clear at all, and your voice just seemed to overlay his and muddle everything up. I know you were saying something to me, but I don't know what."

"And then you woke up," he added. A statement, not a question.

"Yep. Shot up in bed and scared the shit out of Grizz. Poor thing looked like he was ready to tear the bedroom apart looking for whatever threat had come."

"The bear is loyal and brave, if nothing else. I'll give him that."

"He's downright crazy is what he is, but I love him anyway. He gets under your skin in the best possible way. There's no shaking him once that happens."

Merc looked unconvinced. "I'll have to take your word for it."

My expression soured at his reply. "Listen, I get that asking you and Knox to get along is a stretch, but the bear? You can't get on board with the damn bear?"

"I find him to be a tad condescending."

My mouth dropped open, complete and utter disbelief written all over my face as I stared back at the acting vampire king like he had three heads.

"I literally cannot believe you of all people just said that." Another shrug. "You know what? Never mind."

"You're cute when you're flustered."

"And you can be a massive pain in my ass when you want to be."

"I can be many things to your ass," he replied, moving closer to me. I shied away from his approach, not in the mood for those kinds of shenanigans that morning. My head was still a mess about everything that had happened the night before. Joking I could do. Hallway hookups I could not.

"Merc..."

"I understand," he said, pulling away. "It's not a good time."

Although he'd said the right thing, his words belied his disappointment. It was plain in his tone and his body language.

"I'm sorry."

"You don't have to apologize." Awkward silence. "I should go now."

"Merc," I said, catching his arm as he turned to leave. "Do you know anything about what killed Benji? Anything you didn't want to say in front of the others?"

He pinned dark eyes on me and answered.

"No. I don't."

I let out a sigh of relief.

"I wondered if that was why you were trying to reach me last night. I thought I heard an apology of sorts, but I couldn't be sure."

"And that is why you thought I'd apologized?"

When he said it like that, it seemed less probable.

"No?" The upturn in my voice made him smile, if only slightly.

"I have a matter that needs to be attended to at the moment, Piper, but we can discuss this later—perhaps tonight."

"Okay," I replied as he turned to walk toward the foyer. "What do you have to do?" He stopped in his tracks, not turning to face me. Not a good sign.

"I have a loose end that needs to be dealt with."

Loose end... dealt with...

"Merc," I said slowly, stepping closer to him. "Is this about the vampire king?"

His shoulders stiffened. "I will explain things tonight when I come to you."

He disappeared without another word, leaving me with a million brewing questions that would remain unanswered.

6

Time seemed to drag all day, my mind preoccupied with Merc's mysterious words and the looming threat of the fey king's minion. It had been decided that we would resume our search for him that evening, the enforcers working alongside Knox's pack to track down and eliminate the enemy—assuming he wasn't in Faerie. With everything else going on, the last thing any of us needed was some unhinged creature of the fey with a hard-on for picking off Knox's boys running loose. That didn't help anyone's cause, and they all knew it.

For the time being, we would form a united front.

Merc never reappeared, but Jase and Dean handled things in his stead, which made me feel better. Their relationship with Knox and the pack was far superior to Merc's, for obvious reasons. It was easier for everyone involved if they dealt with the pack. Once everything was decided, we split up until the agreed-upon time when we would go after the bastard that had killed Benji.

I wanted to be alone for a minute, but Grizz made that nearly impossible. Thankfully Kat managed to distract him with a bag of chips she was eating in the media room, so I escaped to the kitchen, sitting on the counter in the corner with a cup of coffee and an easing pain in my chest.

I looked up at the sound of approaching footsteps and found Knox standing on the far side of the kitchen, his sad smile saying everything he couldn't. Benji's death had hit him hard. Knox was a fixer—a protector. To have failed at that task on the most basic level was a tragedy I wasn't sure he'd forgive himself for, not that he would ever admit that. Knox didn't do guilt well; he, like Kat, let it morph into something else entirely. In his case, it was revenge. The need for it had been clear in our meeting earlier. But who could blame him for that?

I wanted vengeance for Benji too.

"Hey," I said softly, pushing my curtain of long black hair out of my face. "I made coffee."

"I need coffee," he replied, his sad smile warming a touch. I moved to climb down from the counter and get him a mug, but he waved me off in favor of doing it himself. "You look tired. Did you not sleep well?" he asked, looking at the slightly burnt coffee in his porcelain mug.

"Did any of us?"

"Touché."

Silence fell upon us and I spun my mug in the palm of my hand, not quite knowing how to fill the space between us.

"Knox... I'm sorry about Benji."

"I know you are Piper. You love the guys like family. And they love you."

"Are you, you know...doing okay?"

He pinned narrowed eyes on me. "I will be once we kill the fucker that murdered Benji."

He took a long sip of coffee while his other hand white-knuckled the counter. I could have sworn I heard the marble crack under his grip.

"About that," I started, taking a big sip of my coffee. I wished I'd spiked it because I needed some liquid courage to suggest something I'd neglected to mention at the meeting; something that was undoubtedly going to spike his blood pressure. With Knox, it was best to just throw things like that out at him and rip off the metaphorical Band-Aid. "I was thinking... I know we already have plans to track this guy down tonight with some of the wolves, but maybe it would be better for me to go out alone, or with Jase and Dean, to search for this guy. They can ghost, so they can get me out of there in a hurry if need be, and they're not pack. They won't be targets."

"You can't know that for sure. We have no idea what this guy's endgame is."

"True, but given what you and the boys recognized about him, it makes the most sense that the fey king is after you guys."

"Or maybe he's caught wind of you and wants to get a closer look." He took another sip and swallowed before continuing. "Did Drake sort out the wards?" I nodded. "Good. That should keep him from catching us unaware on the property."

"But beyond that, there is no guarantee. I really think that letting the brothers and me go ahead without a small army would give us a better chance of catching him." He stared at me, unspeaking. "We do need to catch him, Knox. We need to know more about him."

"And how will we contain him? We don't know what he's capable of."

"I will take care of that. If he's fey, we could use iron, right? And if for some reason that doesn't work, I'm sure I can use my magic to encase him somehow. I did bury Kingston at the core of the Earth," I said, smiling over the rim of my mug. "I've got mad skills, you know?"

"That you do." There was a sense of awe in his voice when he spoke that made me blush. It only increased when he walked over to me, leaning against my knees as my legs dangled from the counter. I felt my heart race as he pressed closer, gently forcing my knees apart. As it slammed into my ribcage, I tried to clear my mind, which was clouding over by the second.

"Knox," I said, my voice thinner and breathier than normal. "Why aren't you freaking out right now? I feel like we skipped the part where you tell me how terrible my idea is and how I'm going to get hurt carrying it out. Are you sure you're feeling all right?"

He took a deep breath before leaning his forehead against mine. When he finally pulled away, there was a strange sadness in his expression that I couldn't make sense of. Anger? Yes. Frustration? Been there. But not sadness; not about me doing something he would typically have perceived as reckless.

"Piper," he said, "I am freaking out. I'll always freak out where your safety is concerned. That hasn't changed."

"Then what has? Because I have to tell you, I was expecting a full-blown Knox-style meltdown at my suggestion." I reached out to take his hands in mine. I needed to feel connected to him in that moment—to hopefully feel what was going on with him.

"You've changed, Piper." His reply wasn't an accusation, but there was a hint of anger at that truth. "You've truly come into your powers—just like I knew you would one day. But that puts me in an unusual spot. I'm trying really hard to adapt, but not protecting you goes against every fiber of my being. I'm an alpha. We watch out for what's ours—or try to." The pain in his voice as he said those words made my racing heart still for a moment. "It's more than just an instinct, Piper. It's our purpose in life. But now that you have all that power..."

"You don't feel like I need you."

Silence.

"It's not about *needing* me necessarily. You need me for other reasons. It's more about not wanting to push you away with my knee jerk impulse to protect you instead of giving you credit for the badass you've become." He forced a smile at me, but it was tainted by the sadness he felt. It somehow made me feel worse.

"I'm not a badass all the time," I kidded, hoping to lift his spirits a bit. He let out a tiny laugh, then shook his head.

"You probably could have gotten away with that argument before, but now? No way. Not after what you did to the fey queen. I mean, c'mon Piper, you ripped a hole in the veil between the worlds and snatched Jagger away from that psycho bitch. If that isn't unadulterated power, then I don't know what is... and I'm old as hell. I've seen a lot in my time."

I opened my mouth to argue, ready to cite the other powerful things I'd done before that, but then I remembered that Knox hadn't witnessed them. He'd been unconscious and dying when I buried the warlocks, and he'd been leading our crew toward the portal back to Earth when I killed the fey queen's men. Until the night I'd saved Jagger, Knox had only seen my more rudimentary magic at work.

"You helped give me the power to save Jagger," I argued.

He shrugged off the credit with a shake of his head.

"I amplify what you can do, Piper. But that power... it's all you. And it's more impressive than you'll ever know."

"Are you saying I could kick your ass in a showdown, Knox?" I mused, quirking a brow at him.

That earned me a real laugh, the kind that lit up his blue eyes so bright they almost glowed.

"I'd put my money on you, I think."

"So you're really not going to get mad at me about this plan?"

"I'm not mad about it. I'm not willing to concede to it, though. We have plans to go out as a group, and we'll keep them." I opened my mouth to argue, but he shut me down. "For tonight. With any luck we'll be rid of him tonight, and your plan will be moot."

"And if we aren't?"

"Then we'll do it your way." I tried not to smile at my small victory. "Let me be clear, Piper; I want to be the one to kill this thing. I want to be there when he takes his last strangled breath. And I think I could be of use to you in the hunt, if for no other reason than to amplify your abilities. But the last thing I want is to be a distraction to you—something that makes you lose your focus and gets you hurt somehow..." The unspoken 'or killed' hung heavy in the air between us. "Whether I like it or not, you're far more my equal than someone I need to protect now. And though there will always be a part of me that wants to lock you up somewhere that harm can never find you, the other part—the one that has always craved someone to stand by my side—relishes the idea of you being what you've become."

"Your equal..."

"My better half," he corrected, taking my chin gently in his hand. His thumb brushed back and forth across my lips, lulling me into a state of calm I hadn't felt since I'd rescued Jagger from the fey queen. "Just know that I am trying,

Piper." He leaned in close, his breath warm on my mouth. "For both our sakes."

"I appreciate that," I replied, my words barely a whisper.

"I'm glad to hear it," he said before nipping my earlobe. "I've always wanted a woman that could teach me some new tricks."

"Happy to help," I breathed, my body betraying me. I needed to go, but damned if my hormones weren't telling me to stay.

Then Kat burst into the kitchen, snapping my hormones into line.

"Oh for fuck's sake, you two. This is hardly the time."

Jagger, Foust, Grizz, and Brunton filed in behind her to fan out across the kitchen.

"There's always time for a quickie," Jagger said, grabbing an apple out of the bowl on the counter.

"That's because it's all you're capable of," Brunton countered, snatching it out of his hand. Jagger let out a warning growl, which only made Brunton laugh. "Not my fault that you can't last, my friend." He shot a sideward glance at Kat before taking a massive bite of the apple. "Some of us are just gifted."

"I'm amazed you've managed to get women in bed with you at all," Kat replied. "Did you have to drug them first? Maybe knock them unconscious and then drag them into your cave to have your way with them?"

"Sounds about right," Foust deadpanned.

"Humans are easy," Brunton replied unapologetically.

"And not at all discerning," Kat added just to drive the knife in a little deeper. Brunton only smiled at her slight.

"Sometimes I'm not in the mood for a challenge."

The implied 'but sometimes I am.' hung so heavy in the air around us that I actually started coughing.

"And sometimes I'm in the mood for a quickie," Kat replied, winking at Jagger, who turned nearly as red as his hair. He smiled as he walked past Brunton, lifting his hand to mic drop as he headed for the fridge. He reached in a grabbed a peach out of the drawer.

"That's what I call an upgrade," he said, taking a big old bite out of it and chewing it slowly. Brunton sneered back at him.

"So should we start getting ready for tonight's festivities?" Kat asked, ignoring the shenanigans going on around her. Kat was practically immune to things like that, unless she wanted to partake, of course. In that case, they'd go on until she decided it was time to be done. Her years at the bar had taught her a lot about how to toy with men.

"Is it that time already?" I asked, my eyes darting to the clock on the wall.

Yep. It was.

"Brunton," Knox said, drawing his attention away from Jagger, who was still grinning like an idiot with a cheek full of peach. "Go round up the boys. I'll be out front in a few." He looked back at me and smiled, raking his fingers through his tousled blond hair. "As for your plan, Piper, I have to admit it has merit. I don't like it, but it has merit nonetheless. Let's talk to the brothers about it and see what they think."

For the first time since the fey queen's attack, the pain in my chest totally subsided. My pure joy eclipsed it in a heartbeat.

"Okay!" I replied, shimmying off the counter in front of him. The way my escape forced me to rub against him elicited a mischievous expression from the alpha wolf.

"I should let you have your way more often, I think," he muttered to himself.

"I literally can't with you two," Kat scoffed. "Grizz, let's get out of here before they taint every marble surface in this room... which we don't have time for, by the way." Her words echoed behind her as she exited the kitchen, Grizz following her lead. He stopped just long enough to pin disapproving eyes on me before he too disappeared into the hallway. I tried to stifle my laugh but couldn't. Instead, I let it out—allowing all sorts of tension I'd been holding out with it. The purge felt amazing. Necessary. And sorely overdue.

"We should go," I said, slinking away from Knox's body and heated stare.

I heard him let out a breath as I walked away.

"We should," he finally said, following behind me. "But damn I wish we didn't have to."

7

Our search led us to a part of the city I didn't recognize. What I did recognize was the supernatural energy coming from an alley between two massive old buildings. We were all out and running down there the second the SUV was parked. As we neared, I could sense what we were coming upon. Werewolves. Lots of them.

"Is our assassin among them?" Kat mused as she cracked her knuckles. The wolves, having heard our approach, scattered. The few that remained behind didn't look very friendly.

"What the fuck do you want?" one shouted to us as we neared.

"We're looking for something," Knox said, slowing before we reached the others.

"Like what?" the unknown wolf replied.

"Trouble," Kat said with a wink, flashing a wide smile.

"Looks like you found it, bitch," he said, his boys coming out of the shadows to join him. "You're in our part of the city. And I didn't say you could be."

"I go wherever the fuck I want," Kat replied, stepping toward him. Knox blocked her with an outstretched arm.

"Around here you go where Mack lets you."

"Where is he?" Knox asked with a growl, his attention now on the wolf that had sold Jagger out instead of on the assassin. There would be a heavy price to pay for that mistake.

Before the wolf could reply, he was cast aside by a blur of motion. Then all hell broke loose.

It was inconceivable how fast the attacker moved. In the blink of an eye, he shot through the crowd and dropped two of Knox's wolves in a growing pool of blood. One second, they were poised for a fight; the next, they were dead on the ground, heads severed from their bodies.

As the other pack bolted from the scene, I worked to locate the assassin. Tamping down my fear, I called my magic to cage the beast, drawing on the rage I felt as I looked upon the two corpses. There would be no more. Not if I had any say in it.

"Stop him!" I shouted, firing the words out like I would flame from my hands. For a moment, I thought it had worked. The blur of motion ceased somewhere far from where the melee had started. I ran toward him, but before I got there, a hand shot forth out of the air and dragged him through a slice in the veil just like the one I had created to save Jagger.

"I'll see you soon," a male voice called to me right before the killer disappeared.

"DAMMIT!" I yelled as the din of the chaos died off. Knox and Foust were at the sides of their fallen pack members and I joined them, if only to confirm what I already knew.

They were beyond saving.

"Did you catch him?" Jagger asked, his tone hopeful as he looked around at the mob, hoping to see an unfamiliar face. But there wasn't one to find.

"No, he got away. I was able to stop him, but he had help from across the veil."

"The fey king," Brunton growled as he approached. "I can smell his stench all around here."

Knox was eerily quiet, and with every passing second, it made me more anxious. He should have been a growling, howling ball of anger. But he wasn't. He was too quiet. Too still.

"Knox?" I called to him softly, not wanting to be the one to cause him to snap. But even my coaxing didn't draw him out. He just sat there, his hands on the chests of his fallen boys, not speaking.

Foust looked up at Brunton and then me. Apparently he didn't know what to do either.

"We need to go," Jase said from behind me, taking my arm in his hand. "The wolves—the other ones—we've dealt with most, but some got away. We're in no position to fight right now if they come with reinforcements."

"They're part of the largest pack in the city," Dean added, looking around as though we might be ambushed at any moment. Given our track record, it was a smart move.

"Okay. Get the vehicles and drive them back here." I looked down at where Knox still knelt beside the bodies. "We can't leave them here."

Jase looked like he wanted to argue but didn't, ghosting away with his brother to do as I'd asked. I cast a wary look at Brunton and Foust, their expressions reflecting the concern I felt for Knox in that moment. Something was wrong with him. Something that scared me. Grizz, feeling my anxiety, was at my side in a second, hovering over me like his body alone could shelter me from whatever was to come.

"Knox," I said softly, putting my hand on his shoulder. It tensed the moment I made contact, so I yanked my arm away. Apparently my touch wasn't helping things.

The rumble of the caravan arriving was a welcome distraction. Jase and Dean pulled two of the SUVs up close, hopping out to see if there was anything to help with. But when they got too close to the fallen werewolves, Knox snapped. Big time.

He shot to his feet, golden eyes blazing at them. He lunged for Jase, clawed hand drawn back to strike. Dean drew his blades from the holster at his back, prepared to fight alongside his brother. But Foust, ever the diplomat, grabbed Knox's arm, prepared to face his wrath rather than start a war with the enforcers. He seemed to understand that that was the last thing we needed—that we were stronger together.

Stronger as one big pack.

Jase never flinched at Knox's advance. He stood strong, prepared to weather the alpha's outburst. I loved him so much in that moment; loved how someone born to fight could have such compassion. He knew it had nothing to do with him—that Knox was lashing out because of guilt—but he let him do it nonetheless. And as Foust and Brunton held back their leader, Jase just stood before him, calm as could be.

"I'm sorry for your loss," he said. I could feel the sincerity in his words, and they drew a tear from my eye. Grizz put his hands on my shoulders, grounding me. I saw the fight leave Knox, the tension in his strong, lean frame melting away to defeat. Foust and Brunton clapped him on his back, trying to help bolster his mood, but they couldn't.

He walked down the alley, past the parked vehicles, and disappeared into the night.

"He'll be okay," Foust said, as if reading my mind. I wasn't so sure he was right. In fact, it looked like Knox would be anything but.

"We have to go," Jase said, the urgency in his voice plain.

Brunton and Foust picked up the fallen boys and carried them to the back of the lead SUV. Dean opened the doors for them and stepped back to give them access. As he looked over them to me, I could see the concern in the set of his brow. And Dean didn't let much, if anything, get to him.

Another ominous sign.

Kat, who had remained quiet the whole time, slid up beside me, startling me. I jumped, grabbing my chest as I stifled a tiny scream.

"Jesus!" I said, exhaling hard.

"Sorry. I forget that your hearing isn't like mine."

"I'm going to need you to start remembering that. Like soon."

"No problem." She was quiet for a second, which was unlike her. I turned to see her strained profile. She was looking at something down the alley. She took off in a flash, running down something I hadn't seen. Worried it was the killer, I squealed and took off after her. Foust, Brunton, and Jagger passed me without effort, and Jase and Dean appeared out of nowhere at her side. Pumping my arms and legs as fast as I could, I finally caught up to where the rest of them stood, circled around someone I couldn't yet see.

Or something.

"Well, well, well... what have we here?" Kat said, her words a terrifying purr.

I struggled to push my way through the wall of massive bodies, but once I succeeded, I was met with an unexpected sight—or feeling, as the case seemed to be. At first, it looked like they were all staring at nothing; just the brick wall of whatever building we stood behind. But when I looked closer—leaned toward it—I felt the pull of magic. Fey magic.

"Son of a bitch," I muttered, the words spilling out through my disbelief. "Another portal."

"Bingo," Kat said, stepping closer. I threw out an arm to keep her back. The last thing we needed was for her to be taken to Faerie by whomever was lingering on the other side. "I thought you told Jagger he had help escaping. How did he get away?"

"Someone ripped a hole in the air out of nowhere and snatched that asshole back to safety."

Which, of course, made no sense when there was another means of escape maybe another hundred yards down the alley.

"So why is this here?" she asked, pressing the issue. I wished I had answers for her.

"I don't know."

The group looked frustrated by the dead end. All except for Jagger. He looked terrified.

"Jagger? What's wrong?" I asked, stepping closer to him. I put my hand on his arm, hoping he'd feel better from the contact. But all it seemed to do was make him more tense.

"I smell Mack," he said. "I smelled him on some of the wolves, but here... I smell him here too."

"Shit," Foust bit out, walking back down the alley toward the SUVs. "How deep is that guy in with the fey?"

"I don't know," Jagger said, frustration in his tone. He was desperate to make up for the wrong he'd done, and the fact that he couldn't was weighing on him.

"Can you close this?" Jase asked, thinking of the implications.

"I'll try," I said. "It feels different than the others."

"That's because it doesn't go to the queen," Brunton offered, confirming what I feared; that the fey king also had ties to our side of the veil, and that maybe Mack was one of them.

"We need to get out of here," Dean said, heading back toward the vehicles. All but Kat and Grizz followed suit, leaving us behind to try to shut down the portal looming in the alley. I called forth my magic and uttered a command to seal the portal under my breath. It was met with resistance at first, like the portal was fighting back. But the more I pressed, putting my hand on the amulet hiding under my shirt, I felt the door start to close, blocking the king's gateway to our side. With a loud pop, it snapped closed.

There was no remnant of its power left behind.

"Well done," Kat said, nodding in approval. "Now let's do what the vamp said and get the fuck out of here."

We walked toward the caravan, a weight over us—a nagging sensation that I couldn't shake. The fey king's killer was after something. Something specific. Something he wouldn't give up on. It made me wonder how many more of Knox's boys would be lost in our attempt to bring down the faceless assassin.

I wondered if Knox could survive another.

8

Not surprisingly, Merc was furious when we arrived back at the mansion. He was not happy that I'd accompanied the search party that night. Though I understood that his anger was driven by fear, it still stung. Since I'd returned to the city, he'd never been mad at me. Never raised his voice, not even when I'd nearly destroyed our bond by attempting to kill the vampire king. Since he was normally so calm, his reactions were starting to concern me, especially given our past.

Foust, Jagger, Brunton, Grizz, and Kat stayed close while Jase and Dean tried to lay out what had happened that night in a clinical fashion, hitting the highlights only and leaving unnecessary details out. They didn't want to fuel his apparent anger any more than I did. Once they finished, Merc stayed silent for an uncomfortable length of time. I could feel Foust and the others tense with every passing second. My anxiety made my chest hurt, knowing that Merc was likely to blow when he finally opened his mouth. I wanted to run to my room screaming and lock myself in.

"Piper," he said softly, his voice eerily calm and monotonous. "I'd like to speak to you. Alone."

Kat shot me a look and shook her head. It reminded me of her warning at the bar the night I'd met Merc. My past and my present warred in my mind until I shut it down, deferring to my heart. Though it ached from the mark on my chest, it still believed he wouldn't harm me, so I agreed.

Kat's objection was immediate. "Nope!" she said, stepping from the group to flank me. "You can say it here or you can stuff it, but you're way too on edge to be alone with her right now." Merc cast a sharp glance her way and she simply shrugged. "Sorry man. You made your bed. Now you have to lie in it. I can smell your anger right now, and I'm not letting any of it near my girl."

"Neither are we," Foust added, his calm, unaffected voice belying his growing tension.

I could see the frustration in Merc's eyes. Part of it was aimed at my friends: the rest, at himself.

"Do you share their opinion?" he asked.

I swallowed hard. "No. But you have had a short fuse lately. I know the stress of filling in for the king can't be easy... that you're worried for his safety." I added the latter to keep up the front. "I don't want everyone to fight about this. We've had enough fighting for a lifetime. I don't want to be at the center of it tonight. Or at all."

He nodded. "Where is Knox?"

I hesitated for a moment. "He stormed off..." Panic started to rise within me, and I bolted for the door. "What if the assassin got him?" I shouted, pounding the security code into the pad. Just as it beeped and unlocked, the handle turned and the missing alpha strolled in. He didn't look any worse for wear, but his mood sure hadn't improved. Seeing Merc the second he walked in didn't help. "You're okay!" I said. Throwing caution to the wind, I hugged him, even though he still looked like he wanted to kill someone.

"I'm okay." His reply was unconvincing.

"We put your wolves in the infirmary to be cleaned up for burial," Jase said. Knox looked at him and gave a tight nod.

"Where have you been?" I asked, fearing the answer.

"Hunting." I let that single word lie. I didn't want him to expand on it for fear his response would trigger a war in the foyer. I was worried he'd done something illegal that would require enforcer intervention.

"Oh... okay. We filled Merc in on everything that happened tonight."

"And did he return the gesture? Offer full disclosure on his whereabouts this evening?"

"Why would I need to do that?" Merc replied, eyeing the wolf.

"I just find it curious that the king is missing and you're gallivanting around in his place, covering for him. I wonder if he's really gone, or if he's gone rogue..."

Merc laughed. It held an edge of superiority that was so not helpful.

"Vampires don't go rogue—werewolves do. And as for the king in particular, he is indeed missing, but he is not assassinating your wolves. He doesn't care enough about you or your kind to bother."

"Merc..." I said before Knox cut me off.

"That's because the only thing that asshole cares about is himself—but I'm pretty sure you already know that, don't you?"

"Everyone knows that," Kat said, stepping closer to me. "But for all his dickish qualities, I can't believe the king would kill your boys, Knox."

"You don't think it's strange that this assassin can essentially appear out of thin air, then disappear just as quickly? That we can't track him?"

"Right, but he's hardly going to be mixed up with Mack or the fey king," she argued. "I mean, even that old bastard has standards. And besides, the king doesn't have that ability."

Knox's heavy stare moved from Kat to Merc. "Where is he?" he asked, pressing nearer.

"He is not your killer," Merc replied, evading the question.

Knox just shook his head and started up the stairs. I preferred that to him taking a swing at my mate, but somehow his dismissal seemed to irk Merc more than a physical attack. The vampire disappeared from my side, reappearing at the top of the stairs, right in front of Knox.

"The king is not your killer," Merc said again.

"Unless you can produce him right now, I don't believe it."

"But Knox, Kat's right. Only Merc and his brothers can ghost. Not the king," I argued from the foyer.

Knox looked over his shoulder at me, eyeing me long and hard before turning back to Merc. He took a step around the vampire to stand next to him on the landing.

"Who do you think they got that ability from?" he asked, letting the implication of his words sink in before walking off to the media room. I felt like I'd been hit by the truth train. I stared up at Merc, my face full of disbelief. He did nothing to dispute Knox's claim.

"Holy shit..." It all made so much more sense. Why Merc was next in line. Why he was so enraged by the king's treatment of me. Why he never trusted his leader. He knew the vampire king better than any other because he was his oldest son. His mercenary.

His *heir*.

Realization dawned in my expression and his eyes softened at the sight.

"I could not tell you," he said. "It endangers us all if it's widely known."

"You could have trusted me," I said softly, unable to keep the hurt from my tone.

So many secrets from the men I loved.

"You are right. I should have. But we have other matters to discuss tonight. Pressing ones." He looked to the media room where Knox had just gone and exhaled. "You all should come up here. You will want to hear this."

Kat's gaze fell upon Jase and Dean, her eyes darting back and forth between them.

"So you two assholes are..."

"Second and third in line," Jase said, indicating himself, then Dean.

"How the *fuck* have you two managed to keep that under wraps all this time? You two can't keep a secret to save your fucking lives!"

"Because keeping that secret *does* save our lives," Jase replied. "The fewer people that know of it, the smaller the target on our backs."

Kat let out a sigh of disbelief, and we all filed into the media room. Merc drew the double doors shut and locked them before turning to address the crowd.

"Something has been brought to my attention this evening," he said, daring a glance at me. "I'm still not sure what it means or how it can be dealt with, but it concerns Piper."

"Of course it does," Kat said with a great exhale as she flopped onto the couch.

"Me? What now?"

"What are you talking about?" Knox asked, stepping toward Merc.

Merc pinned his dark eyes on the blond alpha and glared.

"There has always been a relative balance of power among the different breeds of supernaturals. A universal balance that helped keep one from annihilating the others. That, combined with the treaty, allowed us to live in some measure of peace. Now that the treaty is gone, we are left with only that balance to depend on."

"To keep everything from going to shit overnight," Dean added from his position against the wall.

"Your point?" Knox said, pressing the issue.

"My point is that if one of the leaders of any faction falls —without a successor—so does that inherent balance."

"It would create a shit show the likes of which we have never seen," Jase added, coming to stand by his larger brother.

"Precisely."

"But..." I started, working through what he'd said. "That hasn't happened—at least not yet, right?" Merc and I shared a knowing glance before I continued. "So why is this an issue? And what does it have to do with me?"

"For all but the wolves, that successor must be a blood relative."

I stared at him for a second, begging my mind to keep up.

"But wait... that means that... " I cut myself off before I could let loose a truth I couldn't quite comprehend. One that was far more insidious than I could have imagined.

66

"Yes. It does." Merc's reply would make sense to only me in that moment, but it was confirmation nonetheless. We stared at each other until the others began to stir, and Kat finally cracked under the weight of our silence.

"I'm usually not the slow one in the room, but I'm willing to be the village idiot for the day and ask what the fuck you two are talking about."

"The warlock lord." Brunton said from somewhere behind me. I turned to see his expression sharp. "He's dead —and yet there is no imbalance."

I could feel the weight of every set of eyes in that room on me.

"Wait," I said, piecing the puzzle together. "Are you saying that..."

"You are Reinhardt's successor?" Merc said, cutting me off. "Yes. I am." His words nearly knocked me off my feet, and I felt his strong arms wrap around my biceps as my stance faltered.

"So I'm the warlock lord?" I asked, incredulity in my tone.

"Drake said that you were Reinhardt's, did he not?" I nodded. "Do you have reason to doubt his claim?"

"Well, no, but... it's just a lot to take in. I mean, I don't feel any different. Shouldn't I feel different somehow?"

Merc shook his head. "I do not know. That is not how it works for the vampires."

"It is for the wolves," Knox argued. "When an alpha dies, the strongest wolf in the pack takes his place—but he also inherits a certain amount of the power that is lost in death. It's the only way to ensure our strength and survival as a breed."

"Looks like Drake and I need to have yet another chat," I muttered to myself.

"That would explain why he is protecting you," Knox said, walking toward me. "Why he's sticking his neck out for you. He failed Reinhardt. He doesn't want to fail you."

"Yeah... I guess so."

"And why he made sure your man-bear over there can be around you at all times," Jagger added. Grizz, favoring his bear form for that meeting, growled at Jagger. The ginger wolf threw his hands up in frustration. "I don't get why he hates me."

"He hates everyone," Kat said, running her hands through the fur on Grizz's head. "Except for Piper and me, of course."

Jagger scoffed at her and shook his head. Kat laughed in return.

"So if I'm the warlock lord, should I be doing something? Trying to assemble what's left of my kind—if there even are any other than Drake?"

"There are," Jase said, "but they are scattered and unorganized. I have seen a few, but they are skittish. They won't be easily found. You'll need Drake's help if you want any chance at locating them all."

"Why bother?" Knox asked, ever the practical one. "Piper doesn't need them. She needs us. We're her family..."

"Damn straight," Kat shouted from the couch.

"And we'll stand at her side, warlock lord or not."

"You know as well as I do that there is power in numbers," Merc argued. "She will be stronger with her kind behind her."

"She doesn't need more power," Knox said. "She has me for that."

"And when she can no longer handle your amplification?" Merc countered, stepping around me to stand toe to toe with the alpha. "What then?"

"We'll figure that out."

"Will you now? Funny that you haven't lifted a finger to do so."

"You have no idea what I've done for Piper."

"And you have no idea what I'm willing to do."

My lungs suddenly felt like they were in a pressure cooker. The males were mere inches from one another, their expressions tight with rage that threatened to boil over. I could feel the pack behind me, slowly approaching. Whether it was to pull them apart or join in the fight, I wasn't sure, but I damn well didn't want to find out.

I tried to shove my way between them, but it was like trying to shove myself into a narrow mountain crevice. Their bodies were walls of tense muscle that couldn't be budged. I looked over my shoulder at the approaching wolves and found grave expressions on their faces. If I couldn't shut things down, the media room would be the next battleground in the supernatural war.

"That's enough, you two," I said, still attempting to push them apart. Neither one seemed to even hear me.

"Piper," Kat said, a note of caution in her voice. "Remember my toy analogy?"

"Yeah," I said, stepping back from Merc and Knox. I remembered it a little too well. Kat had once told me that things would come to a head between Merc and Knox one day—a fight over their favorite toy. The one they didn't want to share.

"Time to let them sort this shit out... without becoming collateral damage."

A low growl cut through the tension in the room as I backed away from the wolf and the vampire. I bumped into something furry in my retreat. Grizz gave me a stern look as he passed by, stalking toward the two males about to come to blows. In one fluid motion he unfurled his massive body to stand on his hind legs. Then he let out a roar that shook the wall hangings until they crashed to the ground in unison, glass shattering around the room.

That seemed to get their attention.

I couldn't see the look on Grizz's face, but whatever expression it held seemed to shame the rage out of both Merc and Knox. Grizz looked over his shoulder at me and then back at them. He came down with a terrific thud between them, forcing them farther apart before lumbering his way back to my side. He positioned himself so that my hand rested on his back. My fingers ran reflexively through his fur, calming me with every pass.

Merc and Knox looked at me, concern in both their faces.

"I'm sorry, Piper," Knox said, moving to come closer. One lunge from Grizz kept him at bay.

"I, too, am sorry, Piper," Merc said. He didn't bother trying to come near me. He learned from Knox's mistake.

"I think you pissed the bear off," Kat said. I could hear the couch creak as she got up. Moments later, she was at my side. "Might want to check your sheets before you climb into bed tonight."

Grizz snorted, and Kat looked across me to him and smiled. Thick as thieves, those two were. They seemed to be starting a pack of their own.

"There will be no pooping on anyone's bed and that's final!" I shouted, wiping the smile off of Kat's face.

"Buzzkill."

"Now if you two are finished with whatever the hell that just was, we have other matters to discuss... like why Mack is working with the fey king and what this assassin asshole wants." Knox opened his mouth to argue but I shut him down. "As for organizing the warlocks—maybe it's not a bad idea. I mean, if I'm their leader, then they need me, Knox. Just like your guys need you. Surely you can understand that." His frustration faded to resignation. He nodded in agreement. "And maybe they could be of use in catching the assassin. I had him for a moment tonight. I just couldn't hold him. Maybe with their help, I could."

"Let Drake rally the troops," Kat said, her tone unreadable. "You can't be expected to do everything—not with what's going on. And let's not forget the fey queen, shall we? That bitch could pop up at any time."

"Agreed," Merc added. "She'll lay low for a while and nurse her pride. Once she has the perfect plan in place, she'll come back, but not before."

"Great!" I replied, my voice heavy with sarcasm. "One less obstacle for the time being, but that doesn't change the problem at hand." The one that had killed two of Knox's boys earlier. "We need to find Mack. He might be our only lead on this killer, but Knox can't do it. Not with the king's pet out there."

"We'll see what we can find out," Jase offered. Dean stood beside him, nodding in agreement.

"Thanks guys. I'm going to talk to Drake and see what he can dig up," I said. "Maybe I'll search for him tomorrow— hunt someone a little more tangible and a lot less deadly."

"We can discuss it further tonight. *Alone*," Merc said. Judging by the set of his jaw and the tension in his shoulders, he wasn't keen on me going out at all. Especially not after what had happened that night. The weight of his stare was like a vise—it clamped down on my ribs and squeezed until I could hardly breathe. I took a step toward the door, needing to get some fresh air. Needing some distance between us.

With our shaky plan in place for the time being, I headed out of the room. With every step I took, the pain in my chest eased. The stress of everything going on around me was getting to me more than I wanted to admit. I knew there was no way I could live like that much longer.

I couldn't be everyone's hero.

I felt Grizz's breath on the back of my legs as I made my way out of the room. The group was about to disperse, but Kat's voice followed us. The question she posed forced us all to a halt.

"I don't mean to bring this back to Merc's earlier point, but I think this is worth mentioning—especially before you and Drake go out rounding up stray warlocks."

"What?" I asked, desperate for the conversation to be over.

"Has anyone considered that maybe there's another reason why the balance didn't shift with Reinhardt's death?" Everyone turned to stare at her, just as I did.

"What reason is that?" I asked, my voice barely audible as fear snaked up my spine.

"That Drake is a lying sack of shit and Reinhardt isn't actually dead."

Silence fell upon us.

"Kingston said he killed him," I argued, weak though it was.

"And you're willing to take his word for it because he was such an honest guy?"

"What about Drake?" I argued. "He said the same. That Reinhardt is dead."

"Drake is many things," Knox said, stepping toward Kat, "but he is no liar."

"You sure about that?" Kat asked, not faltering under the alpha's approach. "Because you didn't exactly interrogate him that night, if I recall correctly—which I do." Knox's expression hardened. "Next time you see that sketchy fuck, maybe you should try asking him, pointedly, if Reinhardt is dead. Put that annoying lie detector trait of yours to good use." She walked past him, slapping him on the shoulder in a seemingly friendly gesture. But there was nothing friendly about it. "And if he doesn't talk, maybe you should just break his legs and twist them like you did mine. I might not have caved under that tactic, but men are weaker than women. I think you'll find he sings like a canary." She continued on, not bothering to look back and see the shock on our faces as she left the room.

I turned to find Knox standing there, his body coiled with anger.

"Knox?" I called softly.

"She's right," he said. It was then that I knew he was angry with himself, not Kat. She'd pointed out a short-coming in his leadership, and it had stung. "We talk to Drake. *Now*." He looked down at me, eyes glowing gold. "I need you to get him over here, Piper. Do whatever you have to—just make it happen. One way or another, this is getting sorted tonight."

I swallowed hard and pulled out my phone. With shaky fingers, I texted him a message to meet me in the woods right away, that I had information for him regarding the fey king's minion. It was a stretch, but one I knew would make him come at the drop of a hat. Though I did trust Drake, Kat's concern couldn't go uninvestigated. Too much was riding on it to ignore the possibility that my father was out there somewhere, and whatever reason Drake had to keep me from him couldn't override my need for him.

To help destroy the fey king's weapon.

To fill the lifelong void in my heart.

9

With the moon still high in the sky, Knox, Grizz, Kat, Foust, Jagger, and Brunton ventured out into the yard with me, following as I made my way to the woods. It wasn't long before we came upon Drake, standing next to the rickety bridge that he seemed to love so much. When he turned to find me with a small army in tow, his expression tightened and his brow furrowed.

"What news do you have?" he asked, stepping forward to meet our group. "And why have they come?"

"Because you and I need to talk," Knox said, moving through the crowd to stand at my side.

"Do we?" Drake countered, holding his ground.

"We do."

"About?"

"Piper. Mainly about her being the warlock lord."

Drake's eyebrow quirked with curiosity.

"Is there a question in there somewhere?"

"*Is* she the warlock lord?"

A pause.

"No. I am."

I let his reply wash over me. "But that would mean..." My voice trailed off with my thoughts.

"That I am his blood," Drake said, finishing for me.

"*Brothers*," Knox said, realization in his tone. Looked like the warlocks were as secretive about their family trees as the vampires.

"Though Piper would be next in line, she has not yet been called upon to fill my role." He looked at me, his eyes softening around the edges. "Hopefully you're not contemplating my death at the moment so that you can earn that honor."

I choked on a laugh.

"Why didn't you tell me?" I asked him, moving to wrap my arms around his waist.

"I didn't know how you would take the news. I thought perhaps it would be best that you didn't learn that detail for now; that I didn't open up your family-related wounds again."

"Thanks for that, but I think I'd rather have known than not."

"I'm sorry for withholding from you, Piper."

I looked back at Knox, whose expression remained the same. Apparently Drake was telling the truth.

"So your brother *is* dead," Kat said, her weight shifting behind me.

Drake lifted his eyes to her, training them on her sour expression.

"My brother died trying to keep the warlocks together—trying to keep us from severing into two different factions—and he failed. It is now up to me to do what he could not."

"I'll help you," I said softly, pulling away from him. "I'll help you reunite the warlocks."

He smiled down at me, pride in his eyes. "Of that I have

no doubt. Now, do you have something to share about your assassin, or was that just an elaborate ploy to draw me out and interrogate me?" He sounded annoyed, but I could see the tiny curl at the corner of his mouth growing. "Which was well played, I must add."

We quickly filled him in on the attack, the portal, and Mack's potential involvement. Drake listened carefully, his body still. When we finished, he stood silent for a while, contemplating the information.

"It's worse than I thought," he finally said. "And far more dangerous."

"Do you think there's any chance that getting the warlocks to work together could help? I mean, they did against us in Alaska. Maybe we could put that ability to good use."

Drake looked thoughtful. "It's possible. But I need to speak to you about that first." He looked at the group, then back at me. "Privately."

To my surprise, there was no argument from anyone.

"I'll see you inside," Knox said, then followed the others back through the trees until they disappeared from sight. Only Grizz remained behind, not that I'd expected anything else from him.

"What's with the secrecy?" I asked, returning my gaze to Drake.

"The other matter—the one we talked about yesterday. Were you wearing the amulet tonight?"

Oh yeah. That.

"I was."

His face turned grim.

"It's not safe for you to be hunting this being until we know more about what is going on."

"I can't let them go out there without me, Drake. You

haven't seen this thing. It's unlike anything I've ever seen. I was barely able to catch it. They'll die without me."

"And you might die trying to protect them." The heat in his tone as he volleyed his response at me was undeniable.

"Then you and I need to figure this out," I said, softening my tone, "because I have no choice. I can't leave them to do this alone."

Drake exhaled, then looked at Grizz, still in his furry form.

"Stay close to her," he ordered. "Perhaps your connection to her will help recharge her magic." The bear nodded. "Now, Piper, go get some rest. I will do what I can tonight with the warlocks, but I should warn you, bringing them together again will be no easy task. If you are hanging your hopes on their rescue, you may be disappointed."

"Okay," I said, doing my best not to sound exactly that.

"I will see you in the morning."

He gave me a nod, then headed off over the bridge. Halfway across it, he disappeared.

"Shall we head back, big guy?"

Grizz nodded in reply.

I did my best to not let all the unknowns of the evening stress me as we walked back to the house, but it was an impossible task. There was no shaking the undercurrent of terror I felt every time I pictured the fey king's assassin. The image of his shadowy profile was seared into my memory, just like the words that had echoed through the night as he disappeared. *I'll see you soon...* I needed something to wipe it all away.

Maybe Merc hijacking my dreams would be the perfect solution.

10

The morning came with no visit from Merc—in person or in my dreams.

I jumped out of bed, the sun still tucked far behind the horizon, and ran to his room. I knocked on the door with a tad too much enthusiasm but got no response. Grizz, in his furry form, emerged from our shared room to look at me like I'd lost my mind.

"I need to find Merc," I told him. He lifted his muzzle to the air, then lumbered toward me, stopping at Merc's room before continuing. I followed as he made his way down the stairs to the foyer. For a second, his head whipped around like he'd lost the scent; then he looked at the basement door below the staircase. He sniffed wildly as he made his way there, inhaling all around the door. When he seemed satisfied with his tracking, he stood up on his hind legs and pushed the handle down, opening the door.

I could hear sounds from down the stairwell. Sounds of fighting. Before I realized I'd moved, I was halfway down the first flight of stairs. I prayed that it wasn't a showdown between the wolves and the vamps. It seemed unlikely in some ways, but not in others. The tension between the groups was growing. And the disdain between their two leaders wasn't exactly improving either.

Above the basement level with the infirmary was a floor designated for training new enforcer recruits. To my knowledge, they'd stopped training young vampires since the night Kingston and his friends had bonfired me in the middle of Central Park and the treaty had gone to shit. That fact made me even more anxious as Grizz and I approached, the sounds of a battle growing with every step.

I threw open the door to find something other than what I'd feared. The room was full of faces I didn't recognize, squaring off against one another. Around the perimeter of the room were several enforcers, all of whom were staring at me like I'd lost my damn mind. In fairness, I had barged in like a wild animal.

"Hi..." I said weakly, forcing a sheepish smile.

"Piper?" Dean called out, looking through the crowd from the far side of the room. "Everything okay?"

"Yep! Shipshape. I just... um... I was looking for Merc."

"He's not here," Jase said, walking toward me.

"Oh. Well then... carry on." I slinked back out the door and closed it, leaning against it for support. Letting out a breath to steady my nerves, I rested my head against the door and closed my eyes. "Grizz, I think I'm losing it."

"I would prefer that particular affliction not touch you," a dark voice said from the floor below. It drifted up toward me like a song on the wind, announcing Merc's presence. Moments later, he rounded the flight of stairs to stand before me.

Wanting to fluff over what I'd just said, I focused on why I'd gone looking for him in the first place.

"You said you'd see me tonight. I woke up worried that something had happened to you."

"Something did, but nothing like the story you've concocted in your head," he said, stepping closer. Grizz edged nearer, his fur brushing up against my arm where it hung at my side. "Getting you alone is proving more and more difficult these days." He stared down at the bear, who didn't buckle under the weight of it. If anything, Grizz pressed harder against me.

"Well we are rather overrun with extra bodies at the moment."

"Yes," he replied, drawing the word out. "Perhaps a solution to that particular problem will avail itself soon."

I felt the pressure behind those words, subtle though it was. Not so much pressure for me to choose him, although he clearly wanted that outcome. It was more about choosing to go back to normal. Choosing to be rid of the wolves. I couldn't tell if it was my heart or my chest that ached at the thought.

Seeing the emotional battle being waged in my expression, he directed my attention back to the issue I'd raised.

"I'm sorry that I have been unable to see you tonight like I promised. It has been brought to my attention that we may need to resume training enforcer recruits, so I arranged that. I had hoped I could reach you before you awoke, but it seems I've missed that window."

"Well... you could just come talk to me now."

"I am talking to you now."

"Well yeah, but I meant in private."

"You mean without the bear?"

He quirked a brow at me and I felt my cheeks flush.

"Yes, without the bear, but I do mean *talk*."

The eyebrow rose further.

"What a shame..."

Grizz let out a groan of dissatisfaction, then turned to march up the stairs.

"Listen, I wanted to talk to you about tonight—what happened in the alley."

"Was something left out?"

"No, not really. But your reaction when we returned," I said, taking a breath. "You were so angry."

"Because you were out there without me and two in your party died before your eyes. That was not something I enjoyed hearing, Piper."

"I know, but you said you couldn't go, that you had to be elsewhere. What should I have done? Let everyone go without me? If I hadn't been there, God only knows how many more corpses would have been brought back—if anyone had returned at all."

"I think you're exaggerating a touch, don't you?"

"No, I'm not. You weren't there. You didn't see how quickly he took those two wolves down. I did. I was able to freeze him, but he still got away."

"With the help of the fey king or someone under his charge."

"Yes."

"Will you fight the fey king next, then? Perhaps storm Faerie and wage war against him as well?"

"No..."

"Because having one royal fey after you is more than enough, Piper. To court the wrath of two would be suicide."

"I have no intention of thumbing my nose at the fey king. I've got no beef with him directly. But if he's going to keep sending his butchering lackey after the pack, then he and I are going to have a situation."

His lips pulled taut as he assessed just how serious I was.

"I think perhaps you need to spend less time around Kat. She's clearly rubbing off on you."

"Merc," I said, drawing out his name with every ounce of irritation I felt.

"Piper," he replied, taking my face gently in his hands. "All I am saying is that you are not in need of more enemies. Please do not go out looking to make them."

"I can't just sit back and let the boys die." My voice was soft and low and laden with the grief I felt at the losses Knox's pack had already sustained. "Please don't ask me to."

He stared at me, silent, his dark eyes piercing mine. I couldn't tell what was going on inside that head of his, but I knew it couldn't be good.

"I told you once that I would never make you choose between Knox and me, but I never promised not to ask you to you choose between his pack and yourself. I cannot let this go, Piper. Surely you understand why."

"I do, Merc, but for all your talk of being proud of how I survived—became stronger in your absence—you're quick to want to go back to the time when you tucked me away and kept me safe. Either you think I'm capable or you don't. I thought I knew which it was before. But now? Now I'm not so certain."

We stood there awkwardly for a moment until the door at my back bumped into me, knocking me forward into Merc. A very apologetic recruit retreated back into the training room, leaving me standing in Merc's arms. He looked down at me and swept the stray hairs in my face away, tucking them behind my ear as he so often had before.

"I still love you, Piper." His words were so low that, for a moment, I questioned whether I'd actually heard them at all. But then he bent down and kissed me, his lips light and gentle and loving against mine. "Losing you will always be my greatest fear and my greatest weakness."

With that, he pulled away and disappeared back down the stairs the way he'd come. I stepped aside to let the recruits escape before the sun came up, watching them rush out of the room and up the stairs. Jase and Dean were the last to leave. They each cast me a look of concern, but I waved them off. Knowing they didn't really have all day to stand there and interrogate me, they left, although grudgingly. I knew I'd have questions to field when they returned.

And they'd be sorely disappointed by my lack of answers.

11

Since it was early, I thought that maybe I'd pull one of Knox's favorite moves and go outside to watch the sunrise. I would have asked him to go with me, but he still wasn't quite himself since returning from the attack. I thought it might be best to give him a little space.

So, without even Grizz, I sneaked outside and around the back of the mansion to the sprawling patio and flopped down onto one of the cushioned chairs. I folded my legs up under me to keep the chill of the morning air at bay. With my head full of thoughts that I'd rather ignore, I stared off past the trees and waited for the sun to show her smiling face.

Instead, Drake's pensive face blocked my view.

"Feeling any better?" he asked, cutting right to the chase. He reached toward where the collar of the flannel I'd stolen from Dean a year ago gaped open, and I smacked his hand away.

"Excuse me?" I sat up a little straighter, pulling my shirt closed. He dropped his arms to his sides, staring at me like he didn't have time for my shenanigans.

"Your chest? Your magic? Are they better since you've slept? Has it healed?"

In truth, I hadn't had a lot of time to think about it.

"I'm not sure," I replied. "I was able to stop the assassin last night, but I couldn't keep him from getting away..."

Without invitation, he sat down in the chair next to me, turning it to face me.

"I'm just glad you returned unscathed, though I still don't understand why you would go after such a beast when you know your powers are not reliable."

"So I could try out your amulet theory?"

He did not look impressed by my suggestion.

"Piper..."

"Please don't lecture me!" I said, jumping up from my seat. My chest started to seize up at the memory of my quasi-argument with Merc, and I tried to walk it off, rubbing my sternum as I did. "Someone else already did. I'm not sitting through another."

Drake came up behind me and pulled me to a stop. He spun me around to look at him, this time reaching slowly to open the neck of my shirt. The faded blue mark was still there, though lighter. I wanted to believe that the amulet had helped, but I wasn't sure. Yes, my powers had come the night before when I tried to stop the assassin, but were they as strong as normal? I just couldn't tell.

And the pain in my chest didn't seem improved at all.

"What does it feel like?" he asked, his words soft.

"With my powers? Just sort of off in a way. But with this?" I started, pointing at the light blue scar. "I have moments when I don't feel it at all. And then others... I feel like it's tearing me apart from the inside. I can barely breathe."

His brow furrowed and he leaned closer to inspect it.

Then, without warning, he put his hand over it and closed his eyes. I could feel something inside me warm, like I was being jump-started somehow. Maybe my magical battery really had died and that was all it needed: a little spark of someone else's. A little nudge from one of my own.

"You feel the same," he said, unable to hide his dismay. It was clear that he'd wanted his trick to fix me. The fact that it hadn't bothered him—a lot.

"Well since I haven't had a break or less stress or a magical epiphany, I'm not really surprised."

"This is nothing to joke about," he countered, pulling his hand away.

"And it's not something to totally freak out about either. I have the amulet, and maybe, God willing, we'll catch the fey king's minion and my stress level can finally go down."

"Except for the war and the fey queen and whatever other problem chooses to come at you from nowhere."

"Are you trying to make me feel better or worse?"

"I'm trying to make you see reason."

"Good luck with that," I muttered under my breath. His tight expression told me exactly how amusing he found my comment. "You know what might help me? Actually knowing something about my powers. Or my father. Maybe if I knew more, I could help find a solution to what's going on."

He looked like he wanted to argue, then thought better of it.

"What do you want to know?"

I settled back down in my chair and he did the same, staring at me with his wizened grey eyes.

"About my father," I said softly, unable to meet his gaze.

Instead of evading my question, he answered it without pause.

"Your father was an excellent leader. He was powerful but fair. He led by example, not by force, unlike his vampire counterpart." Those words were spoken with great disdain.

"I take it there was no love lost between those two."

"They coexisted. Nothing more."

I remained quiet for a moment, wondering whether telling Drake the truth about the king would only make things worse.

"The vampire king was behind Kingston's move against Reinhardt."

Drake's pale grey eyes practically flared with rage. "Explain."

"The king essentially promised to let Kingston have me if he got rid of Reinhardt."

"Did he now..." Drake's expression of interest couldn't camouflage his growing anger. His rigid posture and flexing jaw gave him away. His control was slipping—and I'd seen what he could do if it fell by the wayside altogether. I wasn't up for that.

"He's going to pay for what he did," I said, taking Drake's hand in mine. "I've made sure of that."

True curiosity overtook his countenance, eclipsing the hatred.

"What have you done, little warlock?"

A smile that would have made Kat proud crossed my face. "Before or after I almost killed him?"

His expression matched mine. "Such a difficult decision... I think I'd like to know the 'during' portion of that story. Did he burn for his sins against your father?"

"In a blaze of ice blue fire."

His smile widened. "You are your father's daughter."

"And because of that, I will avenge him."

Silence.

"Why did you stop?" he asked, moving on to the 'after' portion of my story.

I exhaled hard. "Because killing the king would have forced Merc into his role."

Understanding slowly dawned in the warlock's eyes.

"And you two would be no more... the vampire king cannot have both."

I nodded, feeling my throat tighten around that truth. "Yes."

"And you're not ready to be rid of your bond." A statement, not a question.

"No." My reply was barely a whisper.

"You need not feel shame for your situation, Piper. It is okay to love him still."

"It's complicated," I replied, getting up to walk away from him.

"Your heart belongs to two—that isn't so complicated."

"I'm going to have to disagree on that one," I whispered to myself.

"Piper," Drake said, catching my arm, "your powers—what you are—you are unlike other beings. Convention does not necessarily apply to you."

"So you're saying it's cool if I'm a ho?"

His brow furrowed. "I'm not saying that at all—and that is hardly what you are."

"What am I, then? Because that's a question I'd love to know the answer to, even more than who I should choose." Drake's expression hardened, as though he feared what I was about to say next. "Kingston—the night I killed him—he called me something. A name that I didn't understand at the time, or even now, really. It's like he knew what I was when my powers broke free."

"What did he call you?"

"Fire Bender. But I called myself things after that—like it wasn't even me speaking. Like my power overtook me and spoke on my behalf."

"What did you call yourself?"

"Storm Caller, Wind Walker, Earth Shaker... I listed them all off like they were badges of honor. Like they were titles he should fear."

"And did he?"

"Yep. But not for long. I killed him too quickly."

"Those names... they are the gifts of our kind. We each have one as warlocks. Some of the oldest—like your father and myself—have more than one gift to call, but that took time and power to accomplish."

"So I have more than I should?"

He shook his head. "No, Piper. You appear to have them *all.*"

All of them?

"Oh."

"That is why you have such difficulty keeping them under control when you fully let them out. Our kind wasn't meant to wield so much power at once."

"I know that my mother was part fey," I said softly, admitting to him that I had learned that tiny detail.

His stormy eyes narrowed at me. "Who told you this?"

"Merc."

"And what does he know of your mother?"

I took a deep breath, trying to buy myself a second to collect my thoughts. Merc had told me what he had in confidence. Clearly he was aware of something he wasn't supposed to know, and I wondered, if I revealed too much information, whether I would be endangering him somehow—or my mother, if she were still alive.

"It's complicated..."

"I'll accept the watered-down version. For now."

"Merc was punished for knowing something about the fey queen that he shouldn't have: that she was pregnant with a child not spawned by the fey king. He was imprisoned for eighty years because of it. The vampire king let him out in order for him to determine whether I was born of that child —to confirm that I might indeed hold an immense amount of power—but Merc wouldn't tell him, and everything went south. But he is certain that whatever blood flows through her veins also flows through mine. That much I know." Drake stared at me with wide eyes, unable (or unwilling) to speak. Instead, he turned and walked toward the front of the house. "Drake! Wait! Do you think that's why I have so much power? Is it because I'm of the queen's line?"

"I think I'm going to go drag your mate out of that mansion into the sun."

"Why are you so pissed?"

"Because!" he shouted, wheeling on me. "He should never have told you such a thing."

"Like what? The truth? I would have found out eventually, Drake. Or figured it out for myself. I could feel the pull of fey magic when I went to Faerie. I could feel how it accepted me when I set foot in its lands."

"Knowledge like this is dangerous, Piper. If what he told you is true, and he was indeed incarcerated for eight decades simply for knowing that the queen had a line born of someone other than the king, then how does you being made aware of this help keep you safe?"

"Safe from whom? The queen? Surely she knows she had a baby, Drake. I don't think that's something that can happen without the mother being aware, magical queen of the fey or not."

"But she doesn't know that you are related to her."

"After all I've done to her—all I've kept her from doing —surely she suspects that I'm part fey. That I'm born of a strong line."

He scowled at me but didn't argue.

"She can't be allowed to get her hands on you, Piper," he said, his voice softer and more kind. "She is not interested in getting acquainted with her relation."

"No... she's definitely not. Especially after our last meeting. I think I shit all over that possibility."

"And now you are trifling with her husband." Drake continued on toward the mansion. "I think your mate and I need to talk." He didn't slow, heading for the front door at a blistering pace. "Does the wolf know about your fey DNA as well?" His tone was brusque as he turned on me, piercing me with his angry glare.

"Maybe? I don't remember."

Drake's head lolled back on his neck and he screamed in frustration.

"It all makes so much more sense now," he said to himself, his words little more than a growl.

"What does?"

Again he turned his cloudy grey stare to me. "The queen's actions."

"You think she knows that I'm born of her line?"

"Most definitely. I wonder if we have your mate to thank for that."

The queen's potential knowledge that I was related to her couldn't be a good thing, especially after the lengths she and the vampire king had gone to to keep that news under wraps.

"Shit!" I said, taking off after him. I rounded the corner to find Drake trying to bypass the lock to gain entrance.

"It's not Merc's fault!" I shouted, panic in my voice.

"That is about to be determined," he replied, never taking his eyes off the door as he continued to work.

"What are you going to do?" I asked, approaching him slowly. A storm started to brew above us as my emotions bled from fear to protection. Drake had become a strange but welcome addition to my blended family, but I wouldn't hesitate to go toe to toe with him if he got out of line with Merc, or anyone else that I cared about. He hadn't been around long enough to earn that right.

"Exactly what I told you: get answers."

"Drake," I said, his name a warning. That seemed to get his attention. His hands fell to his sides and he turned to face me. A little of the fire had left his eyes. "You may speak to him, but you may not threaten him in any way. Him or anyone else that knows the truth about my lineage. Got it?"

When he didn't respond immediately, I stepped closer.

"I shall try to contain my displeasure with your mate. Satisfied?"

I considered his response. "Yes. Now, do you want me to just open the door, or are you enjoying your magical workout?"

"Open it," he replied, a clear hint of irritation in his tone.

I let his order roll off my back and moved to unlock the main entrance. I kept Drake away so that he couldn't see the access code, which I planned to change right after he left anyway.

"You think I plan to break in while you're sleeping one night and wreak havoc on this place?" he asked, sounding mildly amused at the thought.

"Not taking any chances."

"You don't trust me."

"I don't trust your temper."

Silence.

"Do you trust your own?"

I looked over my shoulder to find him watching me intently.

"No. I don't."

12

Merc wasn't in his room.

Drake gave me a sideward glare, as though I'd somehow warned him we were coming. Clearly not the case since he was only able to reach my mind when I was unconscious. Dean popped into the hallway from his room as we headed back down the hall. He looked at Drake like he was an enemy for a moment, and my blood flooded with adrenaline.

"What's he doing here?" he asked, coming toward us.

"We need to talk to Merc. Have you seen him?"

"P, seriously. What the fuck is going on?"

Before I could answer, I heard the floor creak behind us. I turned to find Jase looking more ominous than usual as he loomed at our backs.

"I think you should answer the question, Piper." Though his tone sounded less irritated than his brother's, it was clear he didn't like the warlock being in the mansion.

"It's a private matter," Drake replied coolly. "Unless, of course, you've told them as well, Piper. Then the privacy point is moot."

I racked my brain, trying to remember if they knew or not. So many secrets and revelations over a short time were hard to keep track of.

"Told us what, P?" Dean asked, sounding wounded. He never did like feeling left out. Sensitive little enforcer.

I opened my mouth to speak, but Drake's hand on my arm cut me off. Dean's eyes fell to where the warlock gripped me and his expression darkened. Fangs shot forth as he flashed a menacing look at my mentor. I didn't have to turn to see that Jase was doing the same.

Then I heard a familiar growl and felt a brush of fur against my hand. I looked down to see Grizz's massive muzzle wrapped around the warlock's arm, teeth digging into his flesh.

"I would let her go if I were you," Jase said with a humorless laugh. "I've seen the lengths the bear will go to to keep her safe. You don't want to be on the receiving end of that."

"Or me," Dean added, advancing toward us.

"I'm part fey!" I blurted out as Drake released my wrist from his grasp. Grizz, in turn, released the warlock's.

"That's certainly one way to deal with the situation," Drake muttered to himself.

"Are you fucking kidding me?" Dean said, the anger in his expression fading to disbelief.

Jase grabbed my shoulder and turned me around to face him. He stared at me like he could will the whole story from me—or tear my brain open and find it there. But he couldn't; he didn't possess that trait.

"This is why you want to talk to Merc?" Jase asked once he finally found his voice.

"He is the one that told her," Drake replied on my behalf. It was clear that he wanted to stir that pot a bit and saw an opportunity to do so in the boys' ignorance—the fact that their own brother hadn't shared that tidbit with them.

"We just want to talk to him. That's all," I said.

"He's down in the basement," Jase said.

"The infirmary?" I asked, concern in my voice.

"He's fine, Piper. Just needed to talk to Doc about something."

Jase and Dean walked off together, taking their air of frustration with them. They'd always been the ones I'd confided in. They were the first true friends I'd ever had. Now, with all the chaos and turmoil in my life, they were getting lost in the shuffle, and it hurt them. That reality was plain to see. I needed to try harder to stay close to them.

They deserved better.

Grizz, sensing my sadness, pushed between Drake and me and nuzzled my hand. I ran my fingers through his fur to calm myself.

"Basement's this way," I said to no one in particular, leading the way back down the main staircase and around to the door that led down to the infirmary. When we reached the long, sterile hallway, echoes of a memory rang through my mind until the vision of Merc shouting at me— lifting his hand against me—surfaced. I stopped in my tracks, breathing hard like the moment had just occurred. Drake looked at me curiously while Grizz poked his face in mine, trying to determine what—or who—the threat was.

Right on cue, Merc emerged from the double doors at the end of the hall. The fear I'd felt that night was written all over my face when he saw me. He rushed toward me, grinding to a halt a few yards away. It was as if he too remembered; as if he'd put together why I looked so pale and afraid. The shadow of guilt that crossed his face spoke to that fact.

"Piper," he said softly, trying to assuage my fears.

"I'm okay," I replied, doing my best to reassure him. "I just—I just haven't been down here since that night."

"I know. I can see it in your eyes."

He looked from me to Drake, then back again. He was waiting for me to explain why I'd brought the warlock into the bowels of the enforcers' mansion—what could possibly be so important that I would allow him into our home.

"Drake needs to talk to you," I said. "His words, not mine."

"About what?" Merc asked. His irritation was plain.

"You told her she was fey, born of some bastard line. Do you have any idea the danger you've put her in by telling her this?"

"No more than she was already in."

"Fool!" Drake shouted. The walls around us seemed to quake with his anger. "You are as arrogant as your father. At least he has always had the good sense to be paranoid, too." Merc just stared at my mentor, no emotion reaching his expression. That was when Merc was his most dangerous. "Who else have you told about this?"

"Only Piper. It is only for her to know."

"And the king?"

"He has only suspicions, which matter not."

Drake lunged at Merc, stopping only inches from him.

"You think the vampire king won't try to capitalize on that suspicion?"

"He can't." Merc's tone was so final when he spoke those words that they seemed to give Drake pause.

"He is the king of the vampires," he argued, though a considerable amount of heat had gone from his voice. "And there is a war among the breeds. If you think he wouldn't seek to use her against his enemies, you truly are insane."

"I'm not a weapon..." I interjected before I was cut off.

"He cannot use her because he is no longer in power," Merc said, shutting us both down. I looked up at his dark eyes, terrified that he had done something rash—something that could end our bond forever, never to be reforged. Seeing the terror in my expression, he explained. "He is not dead, Piper. That has not changed.

"Piper," Merc said, his expression apologetic. "There is something I must do right now, but I hope to soon bring you peace regarding the vampire king." His eyes fell upon Drake. Suspicion and distrust filled them. "I will go to any lengths to protect Piper." He stepped closer to my mentor, his body seeming to tower over the tall warlock as though he were my height. "And if you prove to be a threat to her in any way, or attempt to sabotage our relationship, I will end you."

With that, he turned and walked back down the long hall to the double doors and whatever business he had behind them.

Drake said nothing, just turned and made his way back up the stairs until he stood before the main door, waiting for me to open it. I did, and the two of us walked outside in awkward silence until I finally broke it.

"I know you think he's endangered me, but I don't believe he has, Drake. And that's the least of my worries at the moment with the assassin running loose killing Knox's pack." I looked into his steely grey eyes. "Will you help us?" I asked softly. "I've made a mess of things where the queen is concerned, but maybe with your help, things won't end as badly with the fey king."

He exhaled hard.

"When are you going after this assassin again?"

"Probably tonight. I haven't seen Knox since he returned

home so I haven't broached the subject. I'm not sure how he'll take the conversation, given the recent turn of events."

"If you suspect that the fey king is after his wolves, then I cannot fathom why you would continually dangle them out there as bait for this creature to eliminate. Knox is fiery and hotheaded, but he's not that reckless."

"Merc might beg to differ about that," I mumbled to myself.

"That is because he is the ice to Knox's fire. They are as opposite as one can find. Their only similarity is their adoration for you."

I blushed, turning away from my mentor in favor of the mansion.

"I think that adoration will ruin them both. They can barely coexist with one another, and that ability seems to wane by the day." I felt Drake's eyes on my face, but I couldn't look at him. It was embarrassing to share that truth with him, to tell him that the pressure cooker that was my love life threatened to destroy us all.

My chest ached at the thought.

I turned to find him watching as I rubbed my sternum in an attempt to abate the pain growing beneath it. The shadow lingering beyond it.

"Make sure you keep the amulet on you at all times. Never take it off. Ever."

"Okay…"

"I mean it. *Never.* Until we can sort this situation out, it remains on your person."

"Got it."

"And as for your fey king's assassin, I will see what I can do. Assemble a group to hunt him this evening—one without Knox or his pack—and I will meet you here. I will hunt him with you."

"I'm not sure Knox will agree to that now," I said as Drake turned to walk into the woods.

"Then make him. Because if you cannot, all he will know until the killer is caught is death."

He disappeared, leaving me with that sobering sentiment. I wanted to play it off as a dramatic attempt to make his point, but it wasn't and I knew it. It was a harsh dose of truth that neither I, nor Knox, wanted to face. For whatever reason, the fey king's creature was targeting Knox's pack, and he showed no signs of stopping. Hand-delivering them to the beast's claws was foolish at best, and suicidal at worst. If we were to have any chance of finding him without losing anyone else, Knox and his boys would have to sit on the sidelines and let the rest of us bring him down.

I knew how well he'd take that reality.

Unfortunately for me, I'd have to be the one to make him see it.

13

L ater that morning I found myself in the vast dining room, hunched over in one of the plush chairs as I rubbed my chest. A meeting had been called to discuss the war and the assassin. The din around me grew as tempers flared, both sides of the table angry about the involvement of the fey king and the potential reasons why. While the wolves and the vampires escalated to near-blows, I zoned out, focusing on the growing pain in my sternum. The faint blue hue peeked out from my collar.

A wet muzzle bumped my arm away from my chest, replacing it with the head of a massive grizzly bear. The concern in his warm brown eyes was plain. He knew something was wrong with me. He just didn't know what.

"I'm okay, buddy," I said softly, leaning my head down to rest on his. I scratched behind his ears and he let out a grumble of approval. "I'm just exhausted and worried. That's all." He pulled his head out from under mine to throw me a dubious look. "Okay, fine. Maybe I need some food, too. That's hard to come by in this house these days."

He looked unconvinced, but rested his head in my lap so I could continue petting him.

"This is the wolves' problem, not ours," someone argued, an enforcer I didn't really know. One I was pretty sure didn't care for me, given the hateful look he gave me before continuing. "It's clear what this thing is really after. Perhaps if we were to force them out of here..."

The poor vamp never even got to finish his sentence before Dean tossed him out of the room. Literally.

"If you want to distance your ass from trouble, be my fucking guest, Asher." Dean surveyed the room to see if anyone shared Asher's sentiments. "That goes for the rest of you too. You want to be pussies, fine. Go do it somewhere else."

Silence had fallen over the room, everyone staring at the vampire enforcer with the big heart and the short fuse. Not one of them seemed to think it wise to challenge him on the issue.

"Thanks, Dean," I said, smiling across the table at him.

"Anytime, P. He was being a douche."

"Agreed," said Jase. "Now, no plan can be made final on our end without the permission of the king—"

"Who's still missing," Dean interjected.

"—so until that happens, we remain in limbo. Releasing the enforcers to help hunt this being is not my call to make." Jase cast a weary glance over at Knox. "My apologies."

Knox nodded at the acknowledgment.

"Am I to assume we're discussing how to proceed with the fey king's assassin?" Merc's voice floated into the room just before he stepped in, his dark eyes searching for me. They lingered once they found me until Jase answered him.

"We are," Jase said. "It has been suggested by one of ours

that we remove the wolves from our midst to rid ourselves of the issue entirely. Dean showed him the door."

"If I can speak freely," Foust said from the perimeter of the room. "Our options seem limited. If the wards are indeed keeping the assassin out, then we can either hole up here or we can go on the offensive, which is sure to cost us more lives. Lives I'm not okay with risking."

"I'm not okay with losing anyone else either," I said softly. "And you guys are not leaving. That's final."

Merc's eyebrow quirked at the finality in my tone.

"We can't be prisoners here indefinitely," Knox replied in frustration.

Merc's gaze drifted to the door and back. His suggestion was less than subtle. Jase and Dean shot me sympathetic glances, knowing just how much Knox's comment had hit home. I'd been all but a prisoner in the mansion before I'd fled; that time seemed so long ago, even though it had only been a matter of a few weeks. I'd needed bodyguards with me when I'd ventured beyond the borders of enforcer land, or I'd suffered the consequences. Sometimes I'd suffered them anyway, even with the boys or Kat at my side.

"We can stand against him," Knox said, looking at me from across the table like I was the only other person in the room. Like he and I were having a private conversation amid the rest. "I know we can do it, Piper. Together..."

"Only if I'm in too," Foust said, stepping away from the wall.

"I'm not getting left the fuck out," Brunton added.

"Me either," Jagger chimed in.

"I cannot allow that," Merc said, breaking through the echoes of the pack, all stating that they were in. Knox shot him a sharp glare and growled. "If you were killed in the process," Merc continued, "Piper would never forgive herself. She would think she was to blame."

"So what's your plan then, Mercenary? Because, like it or not, we can't just strategize and scam our way out of this one."

"Perhaps strategy is a method you should try employing for once, *Trevor*. Reckless abandon has never served you well."

"Maybe not," Knox replied, stepping around the table to face Merc. "Not like cold and calculated has served you..."

"I prefer it to your act-now-think-later method, for which you are famous."

I looked at Knox. His body was tense and rigid, the tight cords of muscle along his neck bulging.

"Yeah... that sounds just like me. Reckless as can be."

Everyone was on their feet at this point, the room primed to break out in a fight at any second. I pushed my way through the crowd to reach the two of them, needing to separate them before the situation escalated further. Grizz cut a path through the bodies until we reached the two men in my life. Like the fearless bulldozer he was, the bear shoved his way between them, forcing them both back a step.

"You two need to stop!" I said, wedging my way in behind Grizz. "You two hate each other—we get it. But that doesn't help us sort this out. You managed to work together in Faerie and when the witches turned on us. Try channeling that for a while, at least until we shut down the assassin. Then you can go back to bickering like old ladies."

A slow clap broke out from the doorway, and I turned to find Kat leaning against the jamb, taking in the showdown. When she knew she had everyone's attention, she pushed off the wall and started toward me, smiling as she always did when she found something morbidly amusing—which was basically everything surrounding the clusterfuck that was my love life.

"Way to go, Piper. I don't think I could have done that better myself."

High praise indeed. "Thanks, Kat."

"I think you all might be interested to know what I just learned while I was out. I may or may not have accidentally on purpose run into Drake—with my car—in the front yard."

"Kat!" I shouted.

"Relax, I barely bumped him. He's fine."

"What did he say?" Knox asked.

"Aside from the few choice four-letter words he spewed at me, he told me that he found out about some underground gambling club in Chinatown hosted by a shady-ass werewolf named Mack." She looked over at me. "He said he sent you a message but you didn't reply, so he came over to make sure everything was okay."

I looked down at my phone, and sure enough, an unopened text notification from Drake looked back at me.

"This is helpful how?" Merc asked, sounding mildly annoyed.

"It's helpful, you fucking grump, because now we know where Mack is. And since we know he is somehow entangled in the fey king's bullshit, he's our best way of finding the killer, or whatever the fuck we want to call that thing." When nobody said anything, Kat let out a put-upon sigh and shook her head. "Why are you assholes not more excited about this?"

"We need details," Knox said.

"And I'm sure Drake has them."

"I'll go see what he knows," I said, heading toward the exit.

"How do we use this to our advantage?" Foust asked. "I mean, it's great that we know where he might be, but we can't go waltzing in there when he potentially knows some of us, and definitely not while this assassin is hunting us down. Hell, he could be lying in wait there."

"That's why we need more details," Knox said again, the annoyance in his tone plain.

"It would be suicide to walk in without knowing more," Merc added.

"Would you look at that!" Kat exclaimed, arms raised. "You two *can* agree on something."

Neither of the males looked impressed with her observation.

"Drake can help," I said, stopping by the doorway. "If he can give Grizz a man suit, then I'm sure he can find a way to protect you or ward you or spell you or whatever to get you into that building to learn what you need to without being recognized."

"And the assassin?" Merc asked, throwing a wrench into my plan.

"Maybe he can help with that too," Knox said, excitement bleeding into his stern expression.

"I'll go talk to Drake. Then we can decide what to do."

"Perhaps while the wolves hunt Mack, we should hunt the assassin," Merc said. "I could accompany you, Piper. Jase and Dean could come as well."

Jase seemed inclined to agree. "He might be drawn to the presence of Knox."

"Not if Drake can protect him somehow."

"I don't care if he can or not," Knox said, leaning forward. "I'm going to find out more about Mack's setup. If I can get him alone, he'll tell me everything we need to know."

"That's a big if," Kat pointed out.

"If or not, it's happening."

"So let me get this straight," I said, trying to piece the plan together. "Knox is going with Drake to hunt Mack while the vampires and I track the assassin?"

"Me too," Kat said, shooting me a scathing look. "I'm going with you."

"Kat, this guy is hunting wolves."

"Wrong. He's hunting *his* wolves," she replied, shooting Knox a sideward glance. "And for copious reasons, which I won't bother going into, I'm not one of his, so I'm going."

"This is the worst plan ever," I muttered under my breath, heading past Kat and the boys to leave. "I'm going to talk to Drake."

"Right behind you," Kat said, following me out. Grizz, Knox, Brunton, and Foust weren't far behind. I could hear the others filing out of the dining room, but I was focused on what Drake would tell us and whether he would be able to do what I hoped he could. There was no way that I was letting any of Knox's boys off the property without some guarantee that they wouldn't be walking targets for the assassin.

Once outside, we headed around the mansion to the back yard. Sure enough, Drake was sitting in a patio chair, looking bored. He stood when he saw us, and, knowing why we'd come, launched right into the facts.

"His place is heavily guarded; I was able to ascertain that much. I have not seen anyone matching Mack's description come or go from the building yet, but I have someone watching it for me. We'll know soon enough if he does."

"Someone watching it for you? Who would you trust to do that? Another warlock?"

He looked at me, mischief in his eyes. "Maybe less of a *someone* and more of a *something*." His eyes drifted to the sky, then back to me. Understanding finally dawned—his raven was on a stakeout. The most inconspicuous of us all. It was pretty brilliant.

"Mack was never known for his subtlety," Knox said, anger clear in his tone.

"Well it seems as though he's grown more cautious in your time away from the city."

"So how do we get in?" Brunton asked.

"The building is warded, which makes things infinitely more complicated. It feels like the coven queen's doing," Drake informed us.

"Can you, I don't know, maybe shield them somehow? Make it so they can't be recognized, or followed by the assassin?"

Drake's mouth pulled to a grim line across his face. "Yes and no. I can do that much while outside Mack's place, but I cannot send them in under that protection. And I cannot go in with them. Her magic will repel me..."

"What? Why?"

His expression grew even darker.

"We have history." I could tell by the way he replied that he had no intention of expanding on his answer or entertaining my questions on the topic. And really, we didn't have time to get sidetracked.

"So you're saying you can't get us in?" Knox asked, reining in his frustration as best he could. I put my hand on his arm and he let out a loud exhale.

"I can get you close, but I cannot send you inside with any guarantee that you won't be found out."

"I'll go," Brunton said. "He doesn't know me. Nobody here should. If anyone can go in unnoticed, it's me."

Kat scoffed. "You? Go unnoticed? Please... you'll start a fight with the first person that bumps into you."

"We need eyes inside," he replied, stepping toward her.

"We do," she agreed, taking a step toward him in return. "Just not yours."

"Afraid you're going to miss out on the action?"

"Hardly. I'll be helping bring down the assassin while you're gallivanting around Mack's den of sin, causing undue trouble."

He smiled at her, a savage twist of his mouth that held no hint of warmth. "Then maybe I should go with you, if you plan to have all the fun tonight."

Kat mocked his expression with uncanny accuracy. "Maybe you should."

Silence fell for a moment before Drake broke it.

"If you two are quite finished, we need to finalize the plans."

"We'll leave you to it," I said, turning to leave. "The brothers, Kat, and I will be out hunting the assassin while you're going after Mack, and we need to fine-tune our own plans."

Drake caught my arm before I could go anywhere. Knox's growl forced him to release it, but he held me in place with his concerned expression.

"You can't," he said. Short, sweet, and to the point.

"We can't leave him on the loose, Drake."

"And you can't stop him," he said, shooting me a knowing look.

"She is more than capable," Knox argued, stepping closer to my mentor. Understanding overtook Drake's expression as he realized that I hadn't told Knox about my power issues. Smart guy that he was, I knew it wouldn't be long before he surmised that he himself was the only one who knew.

"I'll be fine. I'll have Merc, Jase, and Dean with me. Kat's coming too. And Grizz, of course. I'm starting to understand how the assassin operates. I recognize his magic, how he feels. I know I can do this."

Drake's doubtful stare begged to argue. "I should come with you," he said. "We can hunt Mack another night."

"No! We need to do everything we can to stop this thing, and that means tracking Mack down and making him talk."

"She's right," Foust added. "It's a shitty option, but it's the only one we have. We can't leave him to murder at will."

"If you stay here, that won't happen," Drake countered.

"We don't know that," I said. "We still aren't certain that he's only after Knox's boys. What if it's worse than that? What if he's just randomly killing in the city?"

"I've seen no proof to support that theory, but I have not been seeking it out either," Drake said, looking irritated. "And I don't have time to research it tonight."

"Then you guys figure out how to get Brunton into that building without him starting shit. Recon only," I said, my tone firm. "Everyone is coming home tonight unscathed, got it?"

The trio of wolves smiled at me.

"Is that an order?" Knox asked.

"Would you take it if it was?"

His smile widened. "From you, yes. I would."

"Then it's an order."

I walked away to the sound of Foust and Knox laughing and Brunton grumbling to himself. Kat hooked her arm around mine and pulled me in close to her.

"You know that sending Brunton in is the worst idea ever, right?"

"Yep. Sure do. But there's no changing it. We need to know more about the place, and we need to find Mack. If Brunton's the one least likely to be recognized, then..." Kat fell silent as we continued toward the house, Grizz right behind us. "You do think they're going to be okay, right?"

She continued walking. "I think we need to go talk to the brothers."

§🐾

WITH PLANS in place and nighttime upon us, I headed down the hall to meet the others. I hated the idea of splitting up, but desperate times called for desperate measures. I was confident that Drake could protect the wolves from the assassin. The question was, could he protect Brunton from his own temper?

Kat stepped out of her room and looked over at me.

"Are you sure you want to do this?" I asked as I met up with her.

"Oh, I'm sure," she replied. The pack awaited us in the foyer, each one watching as we made our way down the stairs. I could see the concern for us in their eyes, their desire to accompany either search party evident in their stares. "As annoying as these assholes can be, I'm not keen on any more of them dying. Especially not the ginger. He's funny." She winked at Jagger. His cheeks reddened at Kat's comment.

"And Brunton?" I asked. She looked over at me, and I tried to stifle my mischievous smile. She stopped in the middle of the staircase to pin deadly serious eyes on me.

"If anyone is going to kill him, it's me."

I glanced over to where he stood next to Jagger, his expression unreadable.

"So much for your truce, huh?" I said with a sigh. Kat merely laughed at my reply and started down the stairs again. Jase, Dean, and Merc stood in front of the door, waiting. Their expressions were sober and businesslike and didn't give me a whole lot of hope for what the night might hold. I needed Dean to play with his weapons and Jase to smile at the thought of a fight. The tension in the foyer grew with every passing second, and I couldn't wait to escape it.

The wolves said nothing as we walked outside, Knox, Foust, and Brunton following behind us. Drake stood in the front yard as expected, ready to take the trio of wolves to hunt down Mack. I walked over to him, pulling the amulet over my head. His eyes narrowed with every step I took.

"Do you want me to inspect that before you leave?" he asked. His attempt to lead me to the conclusion he wanted —that I should take the amulet for protection—was duly noted.

"I need you to take it," I replied softly. "I know you think you can cloak their identities, but you haven't seen this thing in action. I can't risk having any of you hurt because you didn't have the power to keep him away."

"I have sufficient power to keep the beast from tracking them, if that's indeed what he's doing," he said, pushing my hand with the amulet back toward me. "You need this more than I... unless something has changed?"

I shook my head.

"If that thing's going to help you, Piper, I want you to have it," Knox said, sneaking up behind me. "I won't be there to amplify your abilities this time." I turned to look at him. The worry he felt was etched into his expression, from the furrow of his brow to the grim set of his lips. He did not like our plan at all, but like the equal he wanted to be, he was willing to let me go without him.

Not wanting to out myself, I didn't force the issue with Drake. The last thing I needed was for either of the boys to find out about my magical glitch. I'd never leave the house again if they did.

"Be careful," I said, tucking the amulet back under my shirt. "Both of you."

Strong arms wrapped around me, pulling me into an embrace. Knox held me for longer than necessary, and it scared me a little. It made me wonder whether he thought he might not be coming back.

"You too. Listen to your gut. Protect yourself at all costs," he said, walking over to the SUV where Foust and Brunton waited. They both gave me a wave before climbing in. Drake put his hand on my shoulder and gave it a squeeze.

"They'll be fine. Worry about yourself and finding this creature. The sooner you can put an end to him, the better."

I nodded once, and he walked off to join the wolves on their Mack-finding mission. Seconds later, they were off. I let out a sigh and made my way over to where Kat and the vampires stood, Grizz having joined them while I was talking to Drake. The six of us were as ready as we could be to track the beast hunting those I cared about.

I hoped that night would be the end of it.

Once we were in the SUV, I called forth my magic to see if I could locate the assassin. Within seconds, I knew he was on our side of the veil. The wind whipped up around us, more urgent than when I usually called it forth. That change made me nervous.

Jase sped through the city, following the dusty swirl of wind until we were far from the mansion. Old warehouses lined the road, and Jase made a sharp turn to follow a side street until it reached the retaining wall along the river. The gust of wind didn't disappear, and I sighed with relief. Whatever we were tracking, it hadn't retreated to Faerie. And since I knew it couldn't on its own, I wondered if we finally had the upper hand.

Jase and Dean looked at one another, then ghosted from the car. The rest of us got out and scanned the area. I called the magic, asking if it could draw the creature nearer to us—coax it out of hiding. The wind hovered before me as though contemplating my request, then shot off at an inconceivable speed.

"Is he gone already?" Kat asked, stepping around the SUV toward a warehouse. Then she sniffed the air. "I don't smell anything strange..."

Before she could finish her thought, there was a subtle shift in the air—a spark of magic that felt familiar, but not. I instinctively turned toward its source just in time to see a blur of motion headed for Kat. Just as I opened my mouth to warn her, something slashed across her throat.

"He'll never stop until he gets what he wants," a male voice said, the wind carrying his words.

There was a brief moment when time stood still. When all I could see were the whites of her eyes and the panicked look in them. When everything she and I had ever done together flashed through my mind at light speed. Then the blood started to spill down her neck, and I couldn't stop screaming.

"KAAAT!" Her name stretched out through the silence, smashing it into a thousand pieces. I ran for her as she collapsed to the ground. Kat didn't have the perks of a link to Knox's pack—no power to draw from to keep a fatal injury from ending her. No, she was a lone wolf, and I saw the fear, the knowledge that she couldn't heal fast enough, in her expression as the color drained from her face and the life left her eyes.

I was her only hope.

Just as I dove to the ground at her side, I felt an arm wrap around my waist, pulling me back into a wall of muscle. Then, without warning, I was standing in front of the mansion, still shouting Kat's name. It took my mind a moment to catch up with what had happened. Merc had ghosted us back to the house, leaving Kat behind bleeding to death.

My rage knew no bounds.

"What are you doing?" I cried, wheeling on him. His hard expression never changed. "Take me back!"

"It's too dangerous."

"Take me there now!" I shouted, pounding my hands against his chest. I heard the front door open and knew the wolves would soon be joining us. "She's going to die, Merc!" I could see in his expression that he had no intention of putting me in harm's way, not even to save my best friend. With my belly full of anger, I tried to call my magic. "Make him take me to her," I growled, staring daggers at Merc. But nothing happened.

My magic was connected to the living—and he was not.

"I will never forgive you if she dies," I told him, my voice feral and threatening.

His eyes widened at my words, and then, in a flash, we were standing in front of Kat's bloody body. Grizz was at her side, trying to staunch the bleeding—and failing. Jase and Dean were nowhere to be found.

I ran over to Kat and dropped to my knees on the concrete, the sting of pain pulling me from my terror. I needed to focus. I needed to save her. I'd failed her back in Faerie when Jensen gave his life to save hers.

I would not fail her again.

"Heal her," I said, choking the words out through my tightening throat. I felt a sputter of magic course through me, but nothing like what I normally experienced. Terror like I'd never felt in my life shot through me. "HEAL HER!" I commanded, forcing power into my voice. Again, the spark of healing shot from me, then fizzled out. The wound on her throat had been closed some, but not nearly enough. She was deathly pale, and the rise and fall of her chest was barely visible. I looked over at Grizz with fear in my eyes and he turned to Merc, his lips curling back into a snarl. Even in male form, he was all beast.

"Get away!" I shouted at Merc. When he didn't move, my head whipped toward him. One look at the fury in my eyes and he did as I bade him, retreating enough to give me space. Hopefully it would be enough. I took a deep breath—the way Drake had taught me—and tried again. This time the magic flowed stronger, pulsing through me into Kat. The white light was faint, but present. I didn't need to make her better than normal. I just needed to keep her from dying.

When the light faded, I looked down at her wound. It was sealed but still red and raw, a grim reminder of what we could have lost that night.

Grizz scooped her limp body up in his arms, his head snapping around to look down the alley. I followed his gaze to find Jase and Dean sprinting toward us. I hadn't heard a thing.

"We saw him," Jase announced as he neared. Then he saw Kat in Grizz's arms and reached for her. The man-bear pulled her tighter to him and growled. "We need to get her home," Jase explained, holding his arms out for Grizz to hand her over. He did, but it was clear he wasn't happy about it. Jase disappeared a second later. Dean put his hand on Grizz's shoulder and ghosted him back to the mansion, leaving Merc and me behind. I stared at him, unable to cleanse the angry thoughts from my expression. He read them there, loud and clear.

"I'm sorry, Piper, but I..."

"Take me home," I said, cutting him off. "Just take me to Kat."

With hesitant arms, he wrapped me in his embrace and dematerialized. Seconds later, we were back in front of the mansion. Nobody awaited our return. I ran into the house, calling for Kat.

I blasted into the foyer, looking like a wild beast covered in blood. Finding no one there, I bolted up the stairs, still screaming Kat's name. Jagger appeared on the landing and ushered me into the media room—one of the only rooms in the mansion big enough to hold the entire pack. I entered to find said pack hovering around the sofa, staring down at the person lying on it.

"Kat?" I called. She didn't respond.

"She's okay, Piper," Knox replied, his head popping up amid the crowd. I pushed through the others and climbed over the back of the couch to stand next to him. Kat was sleeping but breathing. Her cheeks once again had color and her respirations looked deep and strong. She was going to be okay.

I let out a huge breath and my body started to shake. My adrenaline crash was massive, and I couldn't hold back my emotions any longer. Tears rolled down my face, and I bit my lip to hold back the sobs that were determined to escape. Knox wove his arms around me and held me tight, murmuring soft words into my hair.

"It's okay," he said, his hands rubbing my back. "Kat's tough."

I nodded against his chest.

"Piper?" Dean called from the entrance to the room. I pulled myself away from Knox enough to look through the crowd at him. "How is she?"

"No longer bleeding to death," I said, trying to force a smile. "So that's a plus."

My attempt at humor did nothing to lighten his expression.

"What I want to know is how it happened in the first place," Knox said, his tone notably harsher than it had been with me.

Jase appeared in the doorway next to his brother, his expression as grim as Dean's. "The fey king's weapon—he attacked her."

"It wasn't an attack," I added. "It was a hit. He went after Kat and then took off."

"We tracked him," Dean said, stepping into the room.

"We *saw* him," Jase corrected.

"But you didn't catch him," Knox replied.

The two shook their heads.

Kat shifted her weight on the couch and all eyes went to her. The interrogations could wait. First, I needed to hear her say something sarcastic and wildly inappropriate. I needed to know she really was okay.

I sat down beside her and pushed the blood-encrusted hair from her face. Her eyes fluttered open and took in her surroundings before she shot up to a sitting position.

"It's okay, Kat. We're home." Her wild eyes seemed to focus on mine, and some of the tension left her body. She opened her mouth to talk, then grimaced in pain, her hand flying to her throat. Apparently I hadn't healed her nearly as well as I'd hoped, and she was too weak to do the rest on her own. "Here," I said, pulling her hand down. I put mine in its place and whispered the words that I hoped would help. A flash of light blazed off her wounds, then disappeared. Kat cleared her throat and gave me a wry smile.

"And here I thought you might relish the opportunity to keep me mute for a while," she said, her voice raspier than usual but functional.

"Tempting," I replied, smiling through my tears.

"Good to have you back," Knox said, reaching a hand out to help her up. She looked at him as though he'd lost his mind, then pushed herself up off the couch to stand in front of him.

"It's good to be back."

"Which of you wants to start explaining what the fuck happened out there tonight?" Brunton asked, parting from the group and making his way toward Jase and Dean. Though the brothers were larger than Brunton, his anger and surly personality seemed to fill the space around him. Neither of them flinched at his approach, but I sure did. I knew if he didn't like what he heard, bodies would start dropping.

"There isn't much to explain," Jase said, stepping closer to Brunton. "Everything was fine until this flash appeared and attacked Kat."

"Fucking coward," Kat muttered aloud. "That 'attack' was the equivalent of being shot in the back. He came out of nowhere."

"He did," I agreed. "I felt this... this ripple in the magic around me, and then I saw the same blur race past Kat. One second, she was fine..." My voice trailed off as I relived the moment when her throat had opened up like a macabre smile. I couldn't force myself to say it out loud.

"The next, I was bleeding to death in the alley," she said, saving me the trouble. Grizz, whom I'd barely noticed since arriving in the media room, let out a growl. He stood up, flanking Kat. She turned and gave him a pat on his broad shoulder. "You kept that from happening though, big guy. Thanks for that."

"Where were you, Piper?" Brunton asked, his tone a touch more civil than it had been.

"I was standing maybe ten feet away. I tried to get to her, but..." Again, I cut myself off, but this time it was for a totally different reason. Revealing that Merc had dragged me from the scene before I could help Kat wasn't going to help things at all.

"I took her away," Merc said as he entered the room. He pushed past Dean to stop in front of Brunton, staring down at him as if daring him to react. But Merc didn't know Brunton like I did—didn't know that his fuse was short and his vengeance unending. The crack of fist meeting face rang out through the room before any of us could move.

"Took Piper *away*?" Brunton repeated, cocking his hand back for another blow. "You left Kat to die?"

"I protected what is mine," Merc said, catching the blow Brunton uncorked on him. He held the wolf's hand captive as he stared him down. Seconds later, Knox launched himself over the back of the couch to land behind Brunton.

"Let him go," he said, the warning in his tone clear. Merc turned to look at Knox, his dark eyes assessing the alpha. There was such condescension in his stare that he reminded me of his father. Had I ever seen that expression on him before, I would have figured out their connection long ago.

Knox, not happy with Merc's lack of compliance, grabbed the vampire's hand and ripped it open to release Brunton. I felt my chest tighten as I looked on. It appeared that their tension was about to come to a head.

Then it didn't. Instead, Kat walked up to the two of them, sliding in between them to face Merc.

"Here's the thing about protecting Piper," she said, staring up at him as though unfazed by his steely gaze. "She doesn't need you to. And if you keep doing it, you'll shoot yourself in the foot. I don't give a fuck that you left me behind to die tonight. You don't owe me anything. But if you had any brain in that hulking head of yours, you'd know that my death would have ruined her in a way that neither you nor Knox could ever make up for. Piper and me... we're tighter than friends. We're *sisters*. So if you do anything like that to hurt her again, dead or not, I will bring pain down on you like you've never felt before."

With nothing left to say, Kat strutted out of the room and disappeared down the hall, leaving everyone silenced by her words.

Knox followed her out, with Brunton and the rest of the pack behind him. After they were gone, only the brothers, Grizz, and I were left—or so I thought. From a dark corner of the room, Drake appeared, walking toward us. His expression was especially grim.

"Did everything go okay?" I asked him, needing a distraction. Preferably a positive one.

His eyes fell to where my hand rubbed my chest. "The werewolf was about to gain entrance to the building when I felt the pull of your magic..."

"You aborted the mission?"

"We went and got them," Jase said, drawing my attention. "We didn't think it was safe after what had happened to Kat."

I forced a smile at him and Dean.

"You say you saw the assassin?" They both nodded.

"Knox and the others will want a description. Maybe they'll know who it is."

"We can do that," Jase replied before hugging me. Dean followed suit, then the two of them disappeared from the room.

"I should join them," Drake said, casting a wary glance at Merc. "I might recognize who the assassin is."

"That'd be great."

Drake didn't move. "Will you be okay if I leave, Piper?"

My chest seized as Merc's temper flared at the question. Drake walked over and pulled my hand away. His eyes skimmed the blood-covered surface quickly before letting me go.

"I'll be fine."

He gave a curt nod, then walked out of the room. I turned to Grizz, silently asking him to leave as well, but he just shook his head. The man-bear had a bone to pick with Merc, and all I could think of was how colorful his language would have been if he could talk. The f-word would have been flying for sure.

"Piper," Merc started, his expression softening as he said my name.

"What you did tonight... you treated me like you did before I could take care of myself. Like you did before everything went to shit."

"I saw certain death and I needed to get you away."

"But at what cost, Merc? Kat's life?"

His eyes narrowed. "If it was a choice between the two of you, then yes."

"But it didn't have to be a choice!" I shouted, frustration taking over. Merc reached for me, but Grizz moved quickly, edging his body in front of mine. Not because I needed his protection, but to make a point. Grizz knew how to navigate that fine line.

Merc, however, did not.

"It's okay, buddy," I said, resting my hand on his back. He looked at me, silently disagreeing, but he had his reasons. Kat was special to him, almost as much as I was. Merc had threatened that connection with his actions. Grizz wouldn't soon forget that.

"I will always put you above all others, Piper. It's my duty as your mate."

I let out a sigh of frustration.

"And I get that, but not like this. Leaving Kat—or anyone else, for that matter—that can't happen again. *Ever.*" I stood there for a moment, hoping to drive home how serious I was. "You'll suffocate me if you don't give me the space I need to become the being I am destined to be." When he didn't reply, I walked past him, headed for the hallway. "C'mon, Grizz. Let's go find Kat. Ten bucks says she's in the kitchen 'refueling'."

The man-bear let out a huff but followed nonetheless. Together we made our way downstairs, following the smell of something delicious cooking.

Though my heart understood why Merc had done what he did, my brain couldn't quite move past it. All I could do was hope that my words had struck a chord with him and he could learn to give me space, just as Knox had. If the over-bearing alpha could manage it, then I saw no reason why the surly vampire enforcer couldn't as well.

14

I saw Merc in my dreams that night. He was in his room, pacing like a caged animal, tugging at his hair. His usual collected demeanor was nowhere to be seen. His focus snapped around the room until it landed where I stood—or where I thought I did. He walked over and stopped right in front of me, holding his hand out to touch me. The confusion in his expression told me what I needed to know. He couldn't see me at all.

I called his name and he flinched.

"Piper?" he whispered, his eyes straining to find me.

"I'm here!" I shouted, waving my arms in front of his face. His hair rustled slightly in the breeze, but still he couldn't find me. With an outstretched arm, I let my fingertips graze his cheek. His eyelids closed as he tried to focus on the sensation. "What's happening?" I asked softly.

"I cannot lose you," he said as though he hadn't heard my question at all.

I dropped my hand from his face, and he resumed his pacing, looking wilder than before. The more I tried to reach him, the more distant and desperate he became. With one final push I lunged for him, screaming his name.

Then I shot awake in bed.

I FLOPPED BACK and lay there for a minute, breathing hard, eyes still closed. I couldn't bring myself to open them yet, my mind and body still clinging to the edges of my dream. It left me feeling unsettled and wondering if it had been a shared dream between Merc and me, or one of my own conjuring. Either way, I knew I couldn't lounge around in bed forever contemplating which it was. No time for that.

When I finally pried my eyelids open to let in the warm morning glow, I found Grizz looming over me, half naked in his man suit. I startled, sitting up quickly. It took a second for my brain to realize that he wasn't a threat.

"Jesus, Grizz... you scared me!" His expression didn't falter. "What are you doing? Is something wrong?" He didn't reply (for obvious reasons). Instead, he scooped me up and set me down on my feet before walking to the bathroom and returning with my toothbrush. "In a hurry to go somewhere?" I asked, taking the toothbrush and shoving it in my mouth. He followed me to the bathroom and hovered close while I finished brushing my teeth. I didn't bother talking to him until I was done. The last time I'd done that, he hadn't seemed impressed.

"I know Drake told you to keep close, but I'm not sure he meant when I'm in the bathroom."

I forced him out so I could pee without an audience. He rolled his eyes as I shoved his massive frame through the doorway. Apparently the grizzly didn't find it strange to stare at someone while they urinated, but I still did. It was hard for my mind to reconcile his human appearance with his animal nature.

As I emerged from the bathroom, he held out a fistful of clothes to me and dropped them into my arms. He looked on as I stripped out of my nightclothes. When I pulled my tee over my head, leaving me in only a bralette for coverage, he walked over. He stared down at the blue marking on my sternum and frowned. His hand drifted up and rested on the mark, covering half my chest in the process.

Then he growled.

"I know, buddy. Drake is still working on it." He turned a sad expression to me, then threw his arms around me and hugged me so tight I could barely breathe. "It'll be okay," I said, my voice more of a wheeze than anything. He let me go but continued to stare at me, concern in his warm brown eyes. "I have you, right?"

He nodded.

I finished getting dressed. The second I was ready, Grizz grabbed my hand and dragged me down the hall.

"Is something going on?" I asked. "Why are you in such a hurry?"

He took the butler's stairs down to the kitchen and continued through the adjoining hall to the foyer. It was as if he was trying to avoid everyone else in the mansion. If I hadn't known Grizz to give zero fucks, I'd have thought he was being sneaky for a reason.

Once outside, he crossed the lawn toward the back of the property. Halfway there, he stopped and sniffed the air, inhaling deep as he let his head roll back, lifting his face to the sky. He looked back at me over his massive shoulder, and that's when I smelled it—the bitter, acrid stench of burning flesh.

We rounded a corner to find Knox and the pack

preparing the fallen wolves for burial. I felt like we were intruding and turned to leave, but a call from Jagger stopped me short.

"Piper—you can come over. It's okay. We wanted you to be here for this. You're family."

I looked at Grizz, understanding now what the hurry was.

"I didn't know," I told Jagger.

He looped his arm around my shoulders and I leaned against him. He was right. He really was family. "Later today, we'll scatter their ashes over the gorge."

"I'm sorry you have to," I whispered, watching the billowing smoke thin as it rose high in the sky.

"We all are," Kat said, coming to join us. She leaned in close to me and whispered in my ear. "I need to talk to you."

I pulled away to find sharp blue eyes staring back at me.

"Okay." We quietly walked away from the group and into the woods, far enough away that we wouldn't be overheard. Whatever Kat wanted to discuss must have been a bigger deal than I thought.

Once we were far beyond the bridge, she stopped walking and started in on me.

"What's wrong with you?" she asked, not pulling any punches.

"Geez, Kat..."

"Something is off with you and I want to know what it is. Maybe these chuckleheads can't see it, but I can. I know you, now spill it." Grizz stood beside me, offering zero assistance where Kat was concerned. Traitor. "I saw you stop the assassin in the alley the other night. But your power... it didn't feel the same. It felt weak somehow. And Knox was there, so I don't know how that could be."

I took a deep breath and pulled my shirt down for her to

see. Her eyes went wide at the sight of the blue mark on my pale skin.

"Something happened after the fey queen attacked us—or at least that's what I think is going on. Drake suspects that my magic healed the amulet, but it cost me some in the process."

Her eyes narrowed. "Will it return?"

I shrugged. "We don't know. He gave me the amulet to wear for now to see if that will help. If I can maybe somehow siphon energy back from it."

"And if you can't?"

Silence.

"Let's hope I can."

"Maybe you just need to go bang Knox until you're fully charged."

"Kat!"

"I'm serious. If that's all it takes, then do it—then do it again right after for good measure."

"You are shameless," I replied, the fire in my cheeks burning for her to see.

"I'm practical. Now, are you sure that's all that's going on with you?" she asked.

"I think so..."

"Is that why you're grabbing your chest all the time? You do it constantly—clutching and rubbing. And you don't look well. You're paler than normal. Again, not really sure how nobody else has noticed." Grizz's chest rumbled with offense. Kat looked at him and sighed. "Of course you have. You're the only male in this place who seems to have a clue."

The man-bear smiled with satisfaction.

"The mark—it hurts."

"All the time?" she pressed, stepping closer. "Because I don't see you do it all the time."

"It seems to get worse when I'm stressed."

"Which is virtually always," Kat countered.

"What are you trying to say, Kat?"

It was her turn to shrug. "I'm just saying I only notice you doing it at certain times. Maybe you should pay more attention—see if there's a pattern."

"Fine," I said, sounding as annoyed as I felt. When I turned to walk away, Kat grabbed me.

"Don't blow me off," she said, sounding hurt rather than angry. A rare thing for Kat.

"I'm not," I said, wrenching my arm from her grip. "And I'll figure it out."

I stormed back through the woods until I was in the yard. Sunshine was there to greet me, a welcome change from the dark and dreary we'd experienced for the past couple of days. I walked to the front yard, leaving Grizz hovering by the entrance. I needed a moment alone. A moment to re-energize. So I flopped down in the grass, arms stretched wide, and let the sun do just that.

"Sunbathing is bad for your skin," a voice called to me from the far side of the driveway.

Drake.

"I don't think melanoma is going to be the thing that kills me," I replied dryly.

"Never tempt fate, Piper. She has a cruel sense of humor."

I looked at him. His approaching silhouette was high-lighted by the sun's golden glow. An aura of magic.

"I wonder if she's related to Kat..." He ignored my comment, walking up the driveway to where I lay in the grass. "Any luck tracking down the remaining warlocks?"

His expression turned grim. "I have found many, but approached none. I'm in a difficult position here, Piper.

Revealing that I am alive and in charge would make me a target. I'm not certain I want to be outed just yet."

I considered what he'd said before replying.

"Would you prefer I do it?"

He shook his head.

"You're an anomaly of sorts. I'm not sure how they will respond to a female warlock, and I do not wish to find out the hard way. But I promise you, I will reunite our kind. It will just take some time to do so."

"And if we need them to take down the fey king's assassin? Or the fey queen? Or someone else, for that matter?"

"Then I will gather them, regardless of what peril it might cause me."

I forced a grim smile.

"I hope it doesn't come to that," I said weakly.

He smiled in return. It was equally empty.

"Do not worry about me. It's you that is struggling. Tell me, are you feeling any better?" Cut right to the chase, that was Drake's M.O.

"Maybe?" I said, pulling the amulet out. I stood up to give it to him.

"That's not an answer. It's a guess."

"I can't tell, Drake. One minute I think maybe I am, then the next I'm doubled over gasping for breath like Grizz is sitting on my chest." I cast an apologetic look to the bear at my right. "No offense, buddy." He didn't bother responding.

Drake reached for the amulet, flipping it over in his hand. "It feels no different." There was irritation in his tone as he spoke.

"Did you expect it to?"

"Perhaps."

"That's not an answer," I countered. "It's a guess."

A wry smile tugged at his mouth. "I suppose you're right. Now about this pain..."

"I'm telling you, it's stress. Non-magic related, good old-fashioned, human stress. That's all. I'm not used to so much riding on me, you know? I used to depend on everyone around me to keep me safe. Now the tables have turned, and I realize what a burden I was to those that loved me. How stressful it is to be responsible for the welfare of another."

"With great power comes great responsibility."

"Yeah... I'm getting a crash course in that."

He was silent for a moment, his head cocking to the side as he looked down at me.

"It's possible that stress could be contributing to this," he said. There was a note of incredulity in his tone, but it sounded hopeful to me nonetheless. Maybe this was more of a human problem than a magical one.

"And if it is? What's the plan, doc? Bed rest? Meditation? A romp in the woods?" Drake looked at me with shock and confusion in his eyes. "No! Not like *romp* romp! Like *walk* romp. Hiking. And not with you! I mean, I could walk-romp with you, but not..."

"Piper!" Drake said loudly, cutting me off to save me from myself. "Stop... please. I understand. Just stop talking."

Awkward silence fell upon us and I toed at the grass, trying not to die of embarrassment. My comment had clearly done nothing to improve Drake's opinion of my love life.

"Seriously, though. What should I do?"

"Though I'm not convinced the matter is this simple, I'm willing to consider it while I seek out another explanation. For now, just take it easy and spend as much time as possible in nature. You've said before you feel as though it recharges you." I nodded. "Good. Then do it." He hesitated for a second, staring at me. "But I would forego the romping."

I threw the amulet at him.

"Dick."

"You asked for my help," he said by way of apology, handing it back. "Perhaps I should go now so that you can rest."

"Okay—but wait. Why did you come?"

"To see how you were doing."

"That's it? No bad news about Mack? Or the assassin?"

His brow furrowed. "I am not the harbinger of all things unpleasant, Piper."

His dark expression suggested otherwise, but I wasn't about to point that out to him.

"Well then, thanks for stopping by." He smiled—as much as Drake seemed capable of smiling—then turned to leave. He strolled back down the driveway, retracing his steps. "Hey Drake?"

He paused to look over his shoulder.

"Yes?"

"Do you have somewhere to go? I mean, you're not really living where Kat and I found you that day, are you?"

The corner of his mouth curled the slightest bit.

"The less you know about that, the better, Piper. But I do appreciate your concern."

He continued to walk toward the edge of the property, disappearing the second he reached it.

"You're welcome," I muttered to myself as I stared at the place where he'd just been standing.

"Have you devolved into talking to yourself now?" Kat asked, sneaking up behind me.

"Not yet," I deadpanned. "Drake was here to check in. He just left."

"Awww... isn't that sweet. The creepy bastard does have a heart buried somewhere under all those tattered clothes."

"So it seems."

"Well good. One less thing to worry about for the moment."

"I feel like that won't put a big dent in the list."

"Nope, but I'm trying this whole positivity thing that's all the rage these days. It's annoying as fuck, but I think I'm just not quite used to it yet."

I looked over my shoulder at her and burst out laughing. "I'm going to need you to stop that immediately. You being positive is a sure sign that the apocalypse is on its way."

She flinched, feigning offense. "That seems a bit harsh, Piper, but if having me be caustic and abrasive helps you have a sense of normalcy, I'm game."

I let out a sigh of relief. "Excellent! Now, I'm supposed to get some rest. Drake's orders. You wanna join me?"

"What are we doing?"

"Just hanging out outside."

Her expression went slack. "That is literally the worst plan ever, Piper. I feel like I've taught you nothing."

She started back toward the mansion without another word.

"Does that mean you're bailing already?"

"No!" she shouted over her shoulder. "It means I'm going inside to get some booze so I can upgrade your shitty plan."

I laughed as she disappeared into the house, knowing that she'd return with a veritable bar in her hands. The downside (or upside, depending on how you looked at it) of living with a bartender. And she did not disappoint.

Minutes later, she returned with two armfuls of liquor. She jerked her head toward the back yard as she made her way there, and I soon followed. Apparently 'rest' meant 'party' to Kat, but I was fine with it. We all needed a break from the craziness around us—especially after Knox had to lay three wolves to rest.

With the sun still in the sky, I helped Kat set up a memorial party for the fallen members of the pack.

15

During our third trip to the kitchen for supplies, Merc appeared. Kat shot me a dubious look before strolling past him out of the kitchen. Grizz, however, didn't budge. Merc stared at him, and for a moment I wondered if they were having a telepathic conversation. Then the man-bear growled at him before advancing, and I knew that, whatever had happened, it hadn't been good.

"Grizz!" I shouted, jumping in front of him. "It's fine. I need to talk to him anyway. Go help Kat... I'll be fine." He looked at me like I'd taken leave of my senses. "I don't care what Drake says. Go!"

With a loud exhale, he headed for the exit, making a point to bump his shoulder into Merc's as he walked by. This time, my mate growled.

"Are you looking for me?" I asked, busying myself with provisions for the party.

"Yes. I need to ask you about last night. My dream..."

"I didn't shut you out intentionally, if that's what you're thinking."

"What did you see?"

I swallowed hard, not wanting to divulge that I'd been essentially sleep-spying on him while he unraveled.

"I saw you in your room. Could you feel me there? You were looking right at me, but you didn't see me."

His lips pressed to a thin line. "I cannot reach you like I once could," he said flatly, his dark eyes narrowed.

I felt my chest burn, and I clasped my hands together to keep them from rubbing and drawing attention to it.

"I haven't been sleeping well enough to let you in, I imagine."

He stared at me. "Perhaps..."

"Is that what you wanted to talk about?" I asked, squirming a bit under the weight of his gaze.

"No. I wanted to tell you that I was wrong to force you to abandon Kat. Can you forgive me?"

I let out the breath I was holding. "Of course I can, but only if you promise to never do anything like that again."

His shoulders relaxed a touch as he took a step closer.

"Drake has been by a lot lately," he said, his tone cautious. "Is it to do with Mack? The warlocks? Or is it something else altogether?"

"He's my mentor—and my *uncle*, apparently. He admitted that the other day. I don't know what it is with supernaturals and family secrets, but it's super annoying."

"Your uncle?" he asked. "I was unaware that Reinhardt had a brother."

"And I was unaware that the vampire king had sired three sons."

He flinched ever so slightly at my jab.

"I did not want to lie to you, Piper."

"I know. But you did. And you're constantly condemning Knox for his secrets even while keeping your own."

"Knox's secrets are plentiful..."

"And yours could be too, for all I know. That's my point. Everyone wants me to take them at their word, even after they're forced to unveil the truth. You guys seriously need to drop some of your shit." I rubbed at my chest, the tension in it growing alongside my frustration. Merc, seeing my discomfort, closed the distance between us in a hurry and pulled my hand away, putting his in its place.

"I will try harder where the wolf is concerned."

"I would believe you if you'd actually used his name and not referred to him as 'the wolf'. Kinda kills the sincerity a bit."

He frowned. "I will try harder with Knox. For you, I can do this."

I forced a smile. "Thank you. Now, I've been wanting to talk to you about this for a while, but time doesn't seem to work in our favor at the moment."

"That is an understatement."

"What about our other problem... you know... the one with your father?"

I felt his hand go rigid against my chest before he pulled it away.

"He is contained for the time being."

"Right, but I mean, that's not a long-term solution."

"It will be for as long as we can keep suspicion at bay."

"But how long do you really think that'll be? Rumors fly in our world and you know it. Someone is bound to suspect me, if not both of us. If the enforcers do, then it's only a matter of time before there's a coup. They'll kill you, Merc, if they think they have to."

"I have taken measures so that this will not happen."

I sighed in frustration.

"And if they fail? What then? I know you're trying to save our bond, but it won't matter much if you're dead."

"It won't matter if you get yourself killed trying to help save the wolves either."

The depths of his dark eyes seemed endless when I looked into them, desperate to find answers to a problem that didn't have any. Somewhere inside me, I knew there were only two ways out of the predicament I'd created. Either we killed the king and broke our bond in the process, or we waited for it all to blow up in our faces. I hated the idea of the former, but the latter would have consequences for sure. The unacceptable kind.

"Where is he, Merc?" I asked, reaching out for his hand. He let me take it.

"It's best that you not know the exact details."

"But how do you contain a being that can ghost? He can do it, right? Or was Knox just bluffing about that?"

"To answer the latter, he was not bluffing," he said, staring down at me. "To answer the former, you use a room created with the sole purpose of imprisoning your offspring should the need arise."

I felt the blood drain from my face.

"Oh, Merc..."

"I have not been held inside of it for some time, Piper. No need to upset yourself over it."

But it was too late; I already had. Whether I did it for him or myself, I wasn't sure, but I wrapped my arms around his waist and buried my face in his chest, squeezing hard. I felt a low rumble in his chest when I did.

"Your father is a monster."

"Not unlike the fey king. The two of them have much in common. This is why I am so disturbed by you hunting the fey king's killer. I know who spawned him. Nothing good can come of this."

"He spawned Knox and the others—sort of."

"He did, but that was back when he still held a sliver of sanity. That broke when Knox escaped. He has been as he is now ever since." My heart sunk further with the knowledge that Knox had been the one to unhinge the fey king. The assassin's mission seemed so much clearer in light of it. "I was detained there to avoid the wrath of the queen. She could have come for me on Earth. In Faerie, she would never dare to trespass on her husband's land. It was the best place to hold me where my father could still have access if need be."

"And he needed you to identify me?"

He nodded. "Such a twisted web he's woven."

I exhaled hard, propping my elbows on my knees. I rested my head in my hands and stared at the male staring back at me. In silence, we just looked at each other, acknowledging without words just how fucked our situation was.

"Do you think he knows who this assassin is?"

Merc nodded. "I believe he does."

"But he won't tell us, will he?" He shook his head. "Is that where you've been disappearing to when you leave the mansion? Trying to get the answer from him?"

"As of late, yes. But as you can imagine, he's trying to leverage the knowledge to gain his release, which I cannot grant."

"Shit..."

"For now, we can hope that whatever information Mack has, your uncle and the others will be able to drag it from him."

"And if not?"

"Then I need to convince my father that I will kill him if he doesn't tell me what I want to know—and be willing to follow through with his execution if he does not."

The sadness I felt at that possibility was plain in the tear that rolled down my cheek. I cupped Merc's face in my hands and leaned forward to kiss him. It was soft and gentle, and my lips lingered against his for a moment before I pulled away.

The desperation of the situation made my chest burn.

"It will be okay," he said, wiping the rogue tear away. "I will do anything for you, Piper."

If only I'd known then just how true and ominous those words were.

16

The funeral for Benji and the others was short and simple, but powerful nonetheless. The sound of a pack's mourning cry was haunting and beautiful, and something that shook the fiber of my being. When it was over, they all made their way back to the house, where Kat's bar was set up and a bonfire was ready to go. Kat and Foust had ripped dead trees out of the ground around the property and dragged them to where the rest of us stood. Grizz had joined in at some point, breaking trunks over his knee like he was snapping kindling. It was effective, to say the least, and before I knew it, there was a pile of wood over eight feet high.

"You want to do the honors?" Kat asked, looking over at the strategically stacked wood.

"Sure," I replied.

I focused my energy, calling forth the blue flames that had served me well. My Fire Bender ability took longer than I expected to come, my fatigue still affecting me, but after a minute, flame shot from my hand, lighting the fire. It burned an eerie, moonlit shade, made more ethereal by the setting sun. I watched it dance and flicker, mesmerized by the calming effect of the movement. Perhaps that was exactly what I needed.

"How's my favorite little arsonist doing?" Jagger asked, draping an arm around my shoulders. I looked up at him, dragging my gaze away from the fire, and smiled.

"Good. How's my favorite ginger doing?"

"Better." His smile faltered for only a fraction of a second, but I saw it nonetheless. Jagger was still struggling with everything that had happened since we'd returned to NYC. He felt like a failure. And he refused to talk about what the queen had done to him in Faerie.

I knew what it was like to want to keep my skeletons in the closet.

I leaned into his embrace and rested my head against his chest. Jagger needed love in the worst way possible, and I could give him that. Forgiveness too, but I'd already given him that. We all had. Apparently he couldn't give it to himself.

"I love you, Jags. You know that, right?"

"I do."

"Good. Now the question is, do you love me enough to go get whatever it is Kat is making over there for me?"

"Can't stop ogling the fire long enough to get it yourself?"

I shook my head. "Drake's orders."

Jagger scoffed. "Only for you, Piper. If you were anyone else, I'd make you go get it yourself."

"Is that so?" Knox said. I could hear the hint of amusement in his tone from behind me, and I turned out of Jagger's hold to see his broad smile as he approached.

"Yes, fine... I'll get you one too," Jagger replied, feigning annoyance.

He walked over to the makeshift bar Kat had set up on the funeral pyre—the one that her mate had burned upon a couple of weeks earlier. To an outsider it would have seemed callous at best, but I knew why she was doing it. It was her way of taking the bull by the horns and throwing that beast right out of the ring. I knew it hurt her to stand there—to have the memories of his death play over and over in her mind—but that was Kat. That was how she rolled.

"About last night," Knox started, his smile fading. "I'm sorry it turned ugly." He exhaled, reaching his hands up to interlace behind his head. "Merc and I..."

"Have too much testosterone for your own good?"

His blue eyes, made bluer by the light of the fire, warmed. "Yeah. Something like that."

"At least you're aware. Knowing is half the battle, or so I've heard."

"Can you forgive me for my Neanderthal ways?"

I considered his words, wondering if his apology would last only until the next time he and Merc were in a room together long enough for a fight to start. There was such a divide between the two of them, which fed the growing divide between the wolves and the vampires in general. The tension level in the mansion was through the roof, and I wondered if we wouldn't implode on our own before the fey king's assassin came for us again. Maybe that was his grand scheme.

It was a genius plan.

"I can forgive both of you for your knuckle-dragging tendencies, but you have to try and find a way to work together. If not for my sake, then for the sake of your pack. Merc as an enemy isn't what you should want."

"He shouldn't want me as one either." Any humor his voice had held disappeared with that statement.

"I don't think he does, Knox."

Knox dropped his arms to his sides and let his head hang back, as if he were asking for the strength to keep his shit together around Merc.

"You're right," he said. "You're right about it all. I promise you I will do everything within my power to keep it together when Merc is around."

I wanted to say something teasing in response, but I held my tongue. I knew how hard it was for Knox to say those words, let alone mean them. I didn't want to make light of it for fear he might take them back.

"Thank you," I said, smiling up at him. Whatever he found in that smile seemed to appease him and his eyes brightened in the failing light of day.

"Your drinks," Jagger said as he approached, holding two massive cups full of God only knew what. We took them from him and moved closer to the fire, winding our way through the pack, who were perched on logs and chairs scattered all around the fire. I found a stump and turned it upright to sit on. Knox found one nearby and did the same, placing it next to mine.

"We used to have these all the time in Alaska," Knox said, staring at the roaring fire. "We'd have smaller fires scattered through the yard to cook on and one huge one in the middle. We'd just sit around it and chill."

"Beers and bros," Jagger said from his spot off to my right.

"We'd use those nights as confessionals of sorts, too," Foust added as he came to sit not far from Knox. "That's how they started, anyway. The fire was a metaphor—a cleansing of sorts for those who felt they needed it."

"When did we start them?" Knox asked Foust, his voice

distant, like he was searching his mind for the answer as he spoke.

"Jesus... I can't remember. I think it was not long after Benji came. Right, Brunton?"

The hard-faced werewolf nodded. "He was having a hard time letting go of his past. Knox decided we should have a bonfire—give him a chance to bond with the pack. Then Knox got up and told his story."

Foust nodded, taking a sip of his drink.

"He sure did..."

"Fuck," Knox said with a laugh. "I forgot about that."

"He did it to show that there would never be secrets among us, and that they would never be tolerated," Brunton said. "That's the moment Benji—and some of the others— knew they'd found their new home. Found someone they could trust. Someone to believe in."

"Because of what Knox shared?" I asked, engrossed in the conversation.

"No," Jagger said softly. "Because he dared to share it." Knox and Jagger shared a look that reminded me of Jase and Dean.

"You were there?" I asked Jagger.

He nodded. "Foust was too. I think that maybe half of us had found our way to Knox by then."

"Do the others know your story too? The ones that came later?" I asked, turning to Knox. "Did you share it every time someone new came?"

He grew still before answering.

"Yes. They needed to know."

A pang of jealousy shot through me at his response. He'd admitted his truth countless times to those loyal to him, but he was unwilling to share the same with me. Part of me wondered if it was because he thought I couldn't handle it. The other wondered if he thought I'd never forgive him because of it.

"Oh."

"Please understand," he started, taking my hand in his. "These guys came to me as broken wolves. They needed to see me stripped down before them—see that I had once been just like them and survived. That was how I gained their loyalty. How I earned it then, and have continued to earn it every day since. They needed to know that I would never ask them to do something I wouldn't do myself. That I would never put my needs above their own."

"I get it," I said, trying not to sound as hurt as I felt.

His expression soured instantly.

"*Lie...*"

Busted.

"You know what I mean. I get what you're saying...it's just..."

"You're hurt because they know things that you don't." I couldn't bring myself to confirm his suspicion, but it hadn't really been a question anyway. He already knew. "Piper..."

"It's fine, Knox."

"Lie."

"I'm just tired and cranky."

"Lie."

"That is not a lie!"

"You're tired and cranky, yes, but that's not the problem at the moment. Piper, you have a right to be upset about this, but know that I want to tell you too—that I plan to—"

"You just can't yet?"

His shoulders slumped slightly and he leaned forward, propping his elbows on his knees.

"It's just different."

"How?"

"Because they came to me—they needed refuge. They weren't exactly in a place to judge me." He looked away from me, taking in the glory of the fire as the sun dipped below the treetops. "And their silence is implicit. They couldn't tell anyone if they wanted to."

I winced at his words. "I came to you for the same reason, Knox. I mean, not intentionally, but still. You have to know I would never tell anyone. Not after everything we've been through."

He hazarded a sideward glance, looking at me through his shaggy blond hair. "You don't know what it is..."

"It can't be that bad," I said, the doubt in my voice cutting through my attempt to hide it. I looked at Jagger, then Foust. Their expressions were less than reassuring.

"What the fuck are you guys talking about?" Kat asked, coming around Foust to join the group. "Jesus, Piper. Drake said to get some rest, not fall into a depression."

"We're talking about Knox's past and why he won't tell Piper about it," Brunton said. "It's a smart move. I wouldn't tell her either if I were him."

"Thanks for that, asshole," Kat snarled. "But next time, raise your hand if you want to speak." Brunton did just that, flipping her the bird. "Actually, just put it down. No more talking for you tonight."

"Wasn't planning on it," he replied, eyeing her tightly.

"So we're finally going to address the elephant in the room, huh?" Kat mused, taking a step closer to Knox. She stopped only a couple of feet in front of him, and he rose to face her—not that I was surprised. "I wonder..."

"Wonder what?"

"Jensen told me something once about the big bad alpha of New York City. The king daddy of all werewolves. He'd never met him; sounded like virtually nobody had, from what he knew. I guess the alpha was a bit of a recluse or something—had trust issues and did most of his work through his second—but Jensen said he'd once heard that he had this ability to discern fact from fiction. Said he'd heard it from some werewolf once, right before Jensen killed him for raping a vampire on the lower east side. That happened long before I met him, though."

"What's your point?" Knox asked, his irritation mounting.

"My point is, I'm standing here with all sorts of pieces to a puzzle, and I can't help but feel like those pieces are starting to fit together."

"Say what you want to say, Kat," Knox dared, leaning toward her.

She didn't budge. "I thought I just did. Do I need to make myself clearer?"

"Knox?" I called, standing up beside him. "Is she right? Is this what you didn't want to tell me?"

"Among other things," Brunton muttered under his breath. Kat and Knox both shot him looks that could have incinerated.

"I thought I told you to shut the fuck up," she said, glaring daggers at him.

He shrugged in response. "I'm a shit listener."

"Anyway!" I shouted, cutting them off before their pissing contest could drag out any longer. "I don't see what the big deal is. So you used to be the alpha of NYC. So what?"

"I don't think it's the position that was the problem," Kat answered for him. "It's what he had to do while holding it that is."

Kat and Knox still stood toe to toe, neither of them willing to be the first to yield. Seeing the futility in the matter, I put my arm around Knox's waist and dragged him away, leaving Kat to smile wickedly in the growing darkness. Once we'd put enough distance between ourselves and the pack to have some privacy, Knox spoke.

"I can't have the others knowing about this, Piper," he said, an edge of concern notable in his voice.

"You mean the brothers? Don't they already know?" He shook his head. "But how? How could they not know this?"

"One of them does…"

I didn't need three guesses to figure out who that was.

"Merc."

"Yep."

"Is that why you two hate each other? Does it have something to do with your time as alpha?"

He shook his head again. "It's more complicated than that. But as far as I know, he is the only vampire who knows who and what I was."

It was my turn to shake my head, but not in negation—in confusion.

"How is that even possible? How can you rule a city full of werewolves and none of them know who you are?"

He was quiet for a minute. "I had help."

"From?"

He took a deep breath. "The fey queen."

Holy shit.

"Jesus, Knox!"

"I need you to understand that my connection to her ended the second I left the city. I've had nothing to do with her since."

"This is why she knows you so well…"

"Yes."

"Why she was so familiar when she spoke."

"Yes."

I turned away from him, putting my hands on my hips to steady myself. "Why wouldn't you tell me this?"

"Because I was afraid if you knew, you wouldn't trust my judgment—that you would think I was somehow still working with her."

"Which you're not."

He looked truly wounded by my words. "Of course I'm not."

I let out a breath. "I just wish you'd told me."

"I know, and I'm sorry. I've spent decades trying to forget who I once was, Piper. Coming back here was an easy choice because of you, but I'd be lying if I said it hadn't torn open a wound at the same time. The person I was when I was here... you wouldn't have liked him."

Brutal honesty at its finest.

"You're not him anymore," I said, my voice taking a gentler tone. "And I don't need to know every detail that the boys do—not if you don't want to share them. But I don't want secrets between us. It hurts us, not helps."

He forced a grin, then took my face in his hands, holding it reverently.

"The voice of reason suits you, Piper."

Leaning in slowly, he kissed my lips. It was a chaste gesture, but it warmed me inside nonetheless. Everything between Knox and me had an intense reaction—from our tempers to our libidos. It was all fire and gasoline.

"We should get back," I said, pulling away from him. My heart and my body screamed at my mind. They seemed less impressed by my new voice of reason status.

"Afraid Kat's going to kill Brunton?"

The thought had crossed my mind. "Or throw him into the fire."

Knox laughed, then put his arm around my shoulders and steered us back to the group.

"I'd pay to see that," he said as we neared the others.

Our spots were still empty when we returned, and we resumed them without a word from the others. The party had gone on without us, and our reappearance didn't seem to affect the vibe at all. I sat back and listened to the boys tell stories of Alaska, and where they were from, and their time before becoming wolves. When it came to that final subject, there was a notable silence from a handful of the wolves, primarily Knox's inner circle. Foust, Brunton, and even sweet Jagger grew extremely quiet during that portion of the conversation. When they saw me watching them, they each got up and made their way over to the makeshift bar. My questioning gaze seemed to offend them somehow.

Before I could overthink that, I heard footsteps approaching. Nighttime had just settled upon us, and I assumed that could mean only one thing: Merc. I looked past Knox, my body tensing at the thought of another altercation between them, but I relaxed a bit when I saw Jase and Dean approaching instead. They stopped a few yards away from the group, looking uncertain as to whether or not to come closer.

"You're welcome to join us," Knox said, waving them over.

The set of their shoulders relaxed a bit.

"We don't mean to intrude," Jase started, coming to stand in front of Knox and me.

"We just wanted to make sure that we all were—you know—still cool," Dean said.

I couldn't help but smile up at the two of them. For all their brawn and badassness, the two of them looked like sheepish little boys about to get scolded. I had to laugh.

"You two crack me up," I said, jumping to my feet. "Everybody's good, right guys?" I looked back at the pack, who turned their collective attention to Knox. He nodded once, and they did too. I turned back to Dean and he let out a breath, then smiled.

"Sweet. I was seriously stressing."

"Drink this and chill the fuck out—and share it with your brother while I make a few more," Kat said, shoving a drink into his hand. "You two are freaking me out with all this emotional shit." She walked between Foust and Brunton, making a point to whack Brunton in the head with her foot as she passed. Foust spit out his mouthful of booze, laughing at how brazen she'd been. Brunton looked unimpressed, staring daggers over his shoulder at the loose cannon headed for the liquor.

Dean extended his newly acquired drink to Brunton. "Dude, I think you need this more than I do."

The gesture only seemed to fuel Foust's outburst, the rest of the pack joining in. Brunton stopped tracking Kat's retreat and turned to eye up Dean. After a second or two, he accepted the vampire's offer and took the cup, slamming the contents of it in a couple of chugs.

"He's going to need more than that," Foust managed to choke out between laughs.

"Good thing Kat has an arsenal of alcohol over there to get him good and liquored up," Jagger replied, laughing just as hard.

"I could use one of those right about now," Jase said with a tentative smile.

"Keep your pants on, fangy. I'm coming," Kat shouted through the darkness to Jase. Seconds later she appeared, carrying more cups than I would have thought logistically possible. They were handed out among the group, and Jase and Dean managed to find places to sit around the fire. The conversation picked back up seamlessly, as if it had never stopped. It felt amazing to have the brothers brought into the fold, finding acceptance amid the Alaskan pack. I felt the tension in my chest ease with every laugh, every joke, every smile.

But there was a notable absence from the party. Merc was nowhere to be found. I kept looking over my shoulder at the mansion, wondering if he was there or if he'd disappeared yet again to interrogate the king. If he had, I hoped he'd get the answers we needed. As much as it felt amazing to have a night off from the chaos, I knew that tomorrow would bring more with it.

Possibly more death as well.

17

"It's only eleven and I already need this day to be over," I grumbled to Kat as we walked down the hall to the kitchen. I pushed the door open and ground to a halt, causing Kat to slam into my back and launch me forward.

"What the..." She cut herself off when she saw why I'd paused. Sprawled out in all his grizzly bear glory was my guardian, lying on the kitchen island dead asleep. It took only a second to figure out why. Empty food containers littered the ground around him as if the marble floor were his own personal trash can.

And it was an impressive amount of garbage.

"Did he eat *everything* in the fridge?" I asked, staring at the paper carnage strewn about.

Clearly in search of the answer, Kat walked over to the commercial-sized refrigerator and opened it. She scoffed and shook her head, which was really answer enough.

"Every last fucking bite."

"The boys are going to be so pissed when they wake up."

"Looks like we'll be eating light today since sending someone on a grocery run is out of the question."

Grizz, still in his food coma despite the noise we were making, snored softly while his right paw twitched. The bastard was dreaming. But not for long.

"Kat," I said, jerking my head toward the pot next to her on the counter.

"Aw shit," she said, smiling like a crazy person as she gave me what I'd asked for. Then she handed me a wooden spoon to complete the set. "He's gonna be so pissed."

She backed away from the island as I lifted the pot and spoon up to Grizz's ear.

"Wake up!" I screamed, banging on the pot like I was trying to wake the dead. A blur of brown fur shot off the island, landing hard on the polished floor. He was on alert, growling as he searched the room for a threat. Then he saw the pot in my hand and narrowed his eyes at me. "You don't get to scowl at me, mister. What you need to do is start explaining this hot mess you've made."

He looked down at the sea of wrappers at my feet and shrugged awkwardly.

"Really? That's all you have to say for yourself?"

"I think he's hung over," Kat observed, toeing a piece of cardboard in front of her. "Or he's acting out."

"About what?"

"You know what," she replied as though it was all the answer I needed. I opened my mouth to argue, then snapped it shut.

"No," I groaned, looking back at Grizz. "Seriously? This is about Merc?" The bear let out a snort at the mention of the vampire. "I know you're upset about the other night, but this has to end between you two. You can't keep doing stuff like this just because you don't like something he did—or Knox, for that matter. Don't think either of us has forgotten the shadoobie incident." Grizz made his weird cough-sneeze sound that I'd come to realize was a laugh. His mockery was so not making things better. "Oh? So this is funny? I don't think you'll find it that humorous when I rat on you to Knox. He and the boys will come looking for food any minute and they're going to find you duct taped to a chair with one of those shaming posters hanging around your neck that says 'I ate my feelings and left remnants of them all over the kitchen'."

"That makes it sound like he shit all over the floor," Kat said with a laugh. Grizz's eyes sparkled with amusement before his mask of indifference returned.

"He'd better not! No poop this time, Grizz! I mean it. Makes me gag just thinking about it."

"I wonder if he has bear-sized shits when he's in his man suit..."

"You are so not helping right now," I shouted, shooting daggers at her over my shoulder.

"I'm just saying... he ate a lot. Has to come out sometime."

"Oh my God! You're worse than he is!"

"Hardly," she said, scooping a wrapper up off the floor. "I clean up after myself when I binge eat."

I heard footsteps coming and shot Grizz a look that told him to run. He lumbered up the butler's staircase as if he didn't have a care in the world, leaving Kat and me to clean up.

Foust and Brunton walked in the room with Knox and Jagger right behind them. The four just stood and stared at the dumpster that was our kitchen. Then they looked up and Kat and me as if we'd been the ones to make the mess.

"You can't be serious," I said, my tone laced with incredulity. "You know we didn't do this, right?"

"Grizz get the munchies in the middle of the night?"

Brunton asked with a laugh. Then he ribbed Foust, who was fighting back his own laughter. "Guess we shouldn't have gotten him that high."

"WHAT?" I shouted, storming toward them. I damn near killed myself when I slipped on a burrito wrapper, but I managed to stay upright with a little help from Kat. "You got my guardian fucked up?"

Foust covered his mouth and turned away, but his shaking shoulders did him in.

"Sorry, Piper."

"Oh, you'll be sorry while you're cleaning up this mess," I said, grabbing him by the arm and shoving him toward it. "You too." I cut Brunton a nasty look, but he didn't buckle under it. Knox, to his credit, said nothing. He'd said he wanted an equal, and it seemed he was using the opportunity to see if the boys would treat me as such. Not surprisingly, Brunton would be the hardest sell. "Let's go. Consequences, my friend."

"I'm not cleaning that," he said, eyeing the mess, then me.

"No?" Kat asked, strutting toward him. She managed to navigate the plastic wrapper minefield far more gracefully than I had. She stopped only inches away from him, her blue eyes boring holes through his. "Let's try this again, shall we? Clean. It. Up."

He leaned closer to her. "No."

Kat spun him around and slammed him into the wall before I could blink.

"I'm starting to think you like it when I rough you up—that you're difficult just so I'll put my hands on you."

"If I wanted your hands on me, I wouldn't have to try that hard."

He flipped their positions as quickly as Kat had pinned him and slammed her back against the wall.

Kat just smiled at him, the expression full of vengeance. "There's a price for touching me," she said, her voice soft and sultry, the tone belying the anger growing within her. "Today it's cleaning the floor."

Brunton laughed and let her go, then walked over to join Foust. He bent over and picked up one wrapper, disposing of it. Then he walked past her and the others and out of the room.

"I'd take that as a win," Knox said, shaking his head.

"Of course it is," Kat said, feigning confusion. "I never lose."

"We need to talk about tonight," Knox said, his expression sobering as he spoke. "We're going after Mack."

"Okay... who's 'we'?"

"Me, Foust, Brunton. Jagger too." He added that final name with a note of hesitation. "He needs to know that Mack won't be a problem for him anymore, and I plan to make that happen."

"What about Drake? Isn't he going" I asked. Knox shook his head. "Explain how that's going to work, then, because he kept you guys from being located last time. You need him!"

"I'm way ahead of you. I met with him this morning—after I stole your phone and texted him to meet me out front. He gave us each one of these." He held up a crystal of sorts. Nothing fancy or even pretty, but I could feel magic pulsing off of them. "He said we had twenty-four hours before their power wears out."

"Why can't he go with you?" I asked.

Knox shrugged. "I think he's trying to help in his own way right now. If we don't need him with us, it's best we let him do his thing. Maybe he's still working on rounding up the warlocks."

"Yeah... maybe," I replied, my mind wandering. Drake had said that the coven queen warded the club. If that was indeed true, then if any of them went inside, Drake's little crystals wouldn't mean shit. That left only one other option. "I'm going too."

"Piper..."

"You're not going without me and that's final. Equals, remember?"

He took a deep breath. "Equals."

"I'm in too," Kat added. "I wouldn't miss this showdown for anything. With all that pent-up rage you have going for you? I can't wait to see you tear Mack's fucking head off!"

"Not before we get answers, I hope," I added, shooting a sideward glance at Knox, who shrugged in response.

"All I know is I want a front row seat," Kat said.

"Don't forget to bring the popcorn," Brunton called before walking back into the kitchen.

Kat scowled. "Do I look like a fucking concession stand to you? Bring your own damn snacks."

Brunton laughed loudly at her response before shooting her a murderous look. I wondered if Mack vs. Knox would be the only showdown that night.

"You won't be bringing any snacks because you're not coming," Knox said, looking at Kat. "This is between the pack and Mack."

"And Piper," Kat added, crossing her arms over her chest. "If she goes, I go. It's just that simple. So I'm going to need one of your fancy little rocks. Hope you got an extra."

Knox shot her a death glare that rolled right off Kat's back. It seemed to make Knox even angrier, which only made Kat smile. I knew she'd never join his pack if for no other reason than she'd have to do what he said, and she enjoyed pissing him off way too much for that.

Seeing the futility in the situation, Knox tossed her a crystal and started for the door. It looked like he'd planned for this inevitability. I giggled a little under my breath, and he looked back at me and quirked a brow.

"Sorry," I said, coughing to cover up my laughter. "Kat just said something funny."

"No she didn't," he replied. "And your laughter only encourages her behavior."

I thought he was actually angry at me until I saw the crinkle at the corner of his eye. He was trying to stifle a smile—and failing miserably.

"She's really not," Kat said, walking toward Knox. "I'm pretty good at encouraging my own bad behavior. I'm an expert at it, actually."

"Meet in the foyer at nine tonight," he said, walking down the hall. "I'm going to go search the rooms for food. And maybe strangle Grizz while I'm at it."

"That'll only make things worse," I yelled after him. He gave a dismissive wave over his shoulder, then laughed.

I hoped his levity would last the night.

"I need to go for a run," I replied, frustration taking over.

"Great. I'll go with you," Knox offered, stopping in his tracks and turning to face me. "I need to talk to you anyway. Alone."

"I'm not really in the mood for a jogging partner," I said, looking back at him.

He grinned. "I'm not really in the mood to be turned down."

"Okay," I said. "You wanna run with me? Fine. But you're going to answer any question I ask while we're gone without argument, got it? And I can run for a really, really long time, so be prepared."

"On those chicken legs?" he replied with a wink. "You'll be lucky to last ten minutes with me."

"Don't worry. I'll make them count." My acerbic tone wasn't lost on him, judging by his expression. He eyed me for a moment, no doubt contemplating whether spending time with me would be worth the interrogation he was about to receive. I quirked a brow at him, folding my arms over my chest. "What's the matter? The big bad wolf scared of a few little questions?"

His lips pushed to a thin line. "I've got to get you away from Kat more often. She's rubbing off way too much."

He wasn't the first to make that observation, but I kept that fact to myself.

"Too late. We're all in."

"I know the feeling," he said, walking past me. "Go get your shoes on."

NOT SURPRISINGLY, Grizz followed us out the door, much to Knox's chagrin.

"Afraid the bear is going to make you look bad?" I joked, tightening my laces before standing up to stretch my arms over my head.

"Hardly," he said, staring at me intently. "It's like a re-enactment of how we all met."

My arms fell to my sides as I remembered my first day at my new Alaska home. I'd gone running in the woods and come face to face with what I'd later come to learn was my guardian, Grizz. A wolf had come out of nowhere and attacked him. What I couldn't have known then was that the wolf was a werewolf coming to save me. Since then, Knox had saved me more times than I could count, both from enemies and from myself. It was so easy to think that all my feelings for him had been superficial—that I'd just been looking for safety with the pack. And in truth, that had been part of my motivation at the time. But I couldn't help but wonder whether, if we'd met under different circumstances, it would have changed anything. Looking up at his earnest blue eyes, I couldn't imagine how it would.

"And look at us now—one big happy family."

"'Dysfunctional' would be a more appropriate term."

I punched him in the arm. "You know what I'm saying."

He took my hand in his, pulling me closer. "It's no coincidence that you ended up in that shitty cabin next to my property, Piper. Surely you see that by now. We were fated to meet."

I couldn't help but think the same could have been said for Merc. I kept that thought to myself.

"Well you're about to be super pissed at fate because I'm going to make the next ten minutes of your life miserable. Tell me again why you agreed to this?"

He started walking off toward the woods in the back yard. "Because you didn't think I would." *Touché.* "And after last night, I figured it was time to bite the bullet and let you all the way in—for better or worse." I looked up at him and smiled. "Questions start the second we start running." He reached down and hit a button on his watch, then flashed me that grin that simultaneously warmed me inside and made me want to slap him. "Question number one...?"

"What finally pushed you to leave NYC?"

"Because I needed to get away."

"Right, but from *what*?"

"From what it was doing to me—turning me into."

"Did you sleep with the queen?" I blurted out before I could think better of it.

He looked over at me as we jogged to the edge of the tree line and shook his head. "Which one?"

So not helping...

"Either of them."

"*No.* Never. But I was hardly a saint before we met—I think you figured as much."

"Well your whole 'gotta scratch that itch' thing was made clear from the beginning."

"Don't forget there was a 'kill something' alternative to itch-scratching. I exercised that one a lot." He looked through the trees and upped the pace as he wound around the massive trunks reaching up from the ground. "You have to understand something about those of us who've been around for a long time—we've had decades, sometimes centuries, to make mistakes. Guys like Merc and me, we've made our fair share."

His point, though I didn't love hearing it, was valid. I'd never exactly asked Merc how many women he'd been with before me. In fact, it hadn't even crossed my mind until then.

"Eight minutes and thirty-five seconds," he announced before pushing the pace even harder. It was hard to breathe let alone think, but I knew it was my only chance to get the answers to some of my questions, so I dug deep and pumped my legs as fast as I could to stay near him.

"What else about your past don't you want me to know?"

"Easy. Everything."

"That's not an answer!" I shouted, gasping for air. I wondered if Knox was trying to teach me a lesson about curiosity killing the cat. I needed a damn inhaler.

"Then ask a more specific question."

"Fine! Tell me how long ago you left the city."

From behind him, I could see his shoulders tense as he ran. He hadn't been expecting that particular question. After swearing under his breath for what seemed like an eternity, he gave me his answer; one I hadn't been expecting.

"About eight decades ago..."

I came to a sudden halt. The grizzly nearly barreled through me, just missing me as he broke through a small tree to my left. Knox, hearing that I'd stopped, followed suit about fifteen yards ahead. There was pain in his eyes as he looked back at me—pain that I couldn't understand but hated seeing. It hurt to even look at him.

"That's when Merc was imprisoned," I said, walking toward him.

"Yes."

"Did you have anything to do with that?"

He looked at me like I'd lost my damn mind. "No! Why? Did he say I did?"

A growl echoed all around us. And it wasn't coming from Grizz.

"No. I just think the timing isn't a coincidence."

He stared at me hard. "Because it isn't."

His words settled upon my mind, making it work overtime to puzzle everything out.

"Wait..." I said, hurrying toward him. "Do you know why Merc was imprisoned?"

Knox's jaw worked hard, his muscles tensing as he considered how to answer my question.

"Not the fine details, but I think I know what got him put away. That's partly why I left."

"You knew about the baby..." My words were barely a whisper.

His eyes went wide at my words. "What do you know of her?"

"I'm asking the questions here," I said, cutting him off. "What do *you* know of her?"

"Aren't we supposed to be running?"

"NO!" I shouted, storming toward him. "Now tell me what you know!"

He exhaled hard, raking his hand through his hair. "I know that she was the queen's bastard child. That psycho husband of hers might as well be neutered, he's so fucking sterile."

"What else?"

"I know that the queen wanted to be rid of her."

I felt ice slide down my spine. "She didn't want it?"

"Of course she didn't. The queen fears anyone and anything with enough power to rival hers. Why do you think her fucking husband has his own half of Faerie to dwell in? It isn't because he snores."

"But she didn't get rid of it. So what changed?"

He laughed, but it was mirthless. "Nothing changed, Piper. That fey bitch wanted the baby dead, but what most beings don't know is that the fey royals can't kill their children—just like their children can't kill them. If she could have, that pregnancy never would have lasted two seconds."

I felt the blood drain from my face. The queen—my ancestor—wanted to kill the line that would eventually create me.

"How do you know this?" I asked, my eyes barely able to meet his. I feared I already knew the answer.

Knox glanced at his watch, then growled. "I told you that the wolves escaped the fey king, but I never told you how. The fey queen helped us. In exchange for this, I promised to owe her a favor to be collected without question when she came to me one day. If I had known then that she would have come to me with the demand she made, I never would have left. I would have stayed in the service of the fey king."

"What did she tell you to do, Knox?" I gripped his arm, and it tightened with every passing second. The need to confirm my suspicion was all-consuming. Instead of shying away from my focused gaze, he met it head on. The self-loathing I saw there broke a piece of my heart.

"Kill the infant."

Time stood still. I didn't move. Didn't breathe. I just stared at him with such disbelief that I wondered if the moment was even happening. "But I couldn't do it. I took the child from her, and I swear, the second I touched it, something in me changed. Nothing was more important to me than keeping that child safe.

"I had a friend on the king's side of Faerie—a friend that owed me a favor. I gave her the child and left. With the baby out of the queen's domain, I knew she wouldn't be able to sense her. To her, I would have done my job. I came back to the queen covered in the blood of a lesser fey I'd killed to keep up the façade, and the second she dismissed me, I returned to New York, packed up my shit, and never looked back."

I felt the tears rolling down my face, but I couldn't bring myself to wipe them away. I was paralyzed by the past he'd just unveiled to me. Something about the way he looked at me told me that he'd never shared it with another. A demon he'd been living with for too long.

The one fueling the darkness within him.

"Knox..."

"I don't want your pity, Piper. I don't deserve it. I may not have killed the baby, but I didn't do right by her either. I didn't take her and raise her myself to know that she'd be okay."

"The queen would have come for you and you know it," I argued, hating to see him in so much pain.

"Maybe. Maybe I could have stood against her on our side of the veil. That's not the point. The point is, I took the coward's way out, and that shit has eaten away at me every day since." He turned away from me to lean his head against the trunk of a massive elm tree. "You once asked me why I took the guys in—why I became a refuge for wayward wolves." I placed my hand gently on his back to let him know I was there. That I was with him still. "It was penance for my weakness. To make up for what I didn't do for that child. I thought maybe if I created a sanctuary for others in trouble, it would make me feel like I wasn't a complete waste."

"You're not a waste, Knox."

He looked over his shoulder at me. "Meeting you is the best thing that has ever happened to me, Piper."

"Only because I excel at courting disaster on a regular basis... and I know how you love danger."

He forced a smile at my weak attempt to break the sadness hanging around us like a fog we couldn't find our way out of.

"True, but that's not the reason." He pushed away from the tree and turned to face me fully. "That first night at the lodge—when you tried to sneak away while everyone was sleeping—you found me outside watching the sunrise. You asked me why I was out there. I told you that watching them was my thing, but I lied." He reached for my face and cupped it in his hand. "I was out there because being in your presence was more than I felt I deserved because I'd figured out who you were."

"You knew I was born of that child you saved."

"I knew that the baby had lived, and I felt like a weight had been lifted from my heart, Piper. Like, in addition to our magical connection, there was something deeper between us. I knew in my soul that we were meant to be together. I hate the circumstances that drove us together, but I will never regret following you through the woods while you ran or giving you refuge or losing everything to the warlocks. Hell, I'd have died a happy man that night knowing that I'd protected you." I winced at the memory of his life fading away while I held him in my arms. I tried to shake it off, but it lingered still. Knox, observant as always, saw my thoughts written in my expression and pulled me into his arms, holding me tight. "I know that you feel guilty for your situation right now, Piper, but you don't need to. Just know that I love you for you—not just because of this bond we have. I love you for who you are and who you're becoming. I've always known you were capable of reaching your magic. You just needed a little help."

He let me go and swept his arms wide as if to take credit for being the push my magic needed. I couldn't help but laugh. Even in tense times, Knox always knew how to lift me up—how to pull me from the depths.

"Yes, thanks for that. Maybe next time don't almost die to make that happen."

"I can get on board with that plan. Death doesn't really suit me." He gave me a wink, then pulled me back into his arms.

Then his timer started beeping in my ear, and I knew my interrogation was over.

"Had enough truth for one day?" he asked. "Or do you want to quiz me some more on my past love life?"

I choked on a laugh.

"Nope. All set with that. Thanks."

"Well then, should we finish our run or call it a day?"

"I think I'm all set with physical activity at the moment."

Knox feigned a pout. "That's unfortunate."

"You're incorrigible."

"Big word there, chicken legs. Must be hard to balance that big old brain on those skinny things."

"I do not have chicken legs!" I shouted in mock frustration. "And I'll show you balance..."

I muttered a few words under my breath and a massive root shot up from the ground, knocking Knox's feet out from under him. I took off in a mad sprint, giggling as I did. I knew I was toast the second he caught up to me—he'd said as much as I ran away—but I didn't care. The look on his face had been well worth it.

I could hear him gaining on me, and I looked forward to being tackled by the alpha wolf who'd saved that child from being murdered and exterminating my line. A part of me—the real, non-magical me—loved being around him. Even at his grumpiest, there was a realness to Knox that I loved. He was who he was without pretense. And now, with his tightly guarded past revealed, I felt it even more. There was freedom in the truth, painful though it may be.

There was comfort in overcoming our demons.

18

Jase came to my room later that afternoon. He shut and locked the door behind him before ushering me into my bathroom and closing that door too.

"Piper, have you talked to Merc today?"

"No," I said, anxiety starting to rise within me. "Why?"

"Because he's not here. He never came back last night."

"Can't you reach him? You know... with your mind?"

"No, which has me worried."

"Did you call him?"

"Nothing..."

Shit.

"Jase... do you know where your father is?"

He looked at me in confusion until realization dawned in his expression.

"You think he has something to do with his disappearance..."

"No. I know he does. I did something I shouldn't have, and Merc cleaned up my mess."

Sympathetic eyes met mine. "This isn't good, Piper."

"I know that," I whispered. "But I'm confident he's okay.

He said something about a room your father had built to contain any of you three if he needed to. He didn't say where it was, but my guess is that if it can block your ghosting abilities, then it can block your mental abilities too."

"Yeah," he said, his voice and gaze suddenly distant. "Yeah... that sounds reasonable. I'm going to go tell Dean..."

"You okay, Jase?"

He nodded, forcing a smile for good measure. But it never reached his eyes.

"I'll see you later, Piper."

"Actually, I'm heading out with Knox and some of the guys to find Mack."

His eyes snapped into focus. "We're coming with you."

"No. There's no way you're getting into that club undetected, Jase. And if word gets out that enforcers are there, Mack will bail. We can't afford that."

"So what's your plan?"

I swallowed hard. "I'm not sure yet, but it'll be fine. If anything goes wrong, I'll just burn the place down, okay?" I smiled at him, trying to bait him into a better mood. It failed miserably.

"I don't like this, Piper. I want to help, but I feel like you don't want me to."

"It's not that, Jase. I just... I need you to find Merc. Make sure he doesn't do anything *irreversible* where the king is concerned. Understand?"

The sad look in his eyes told me he did. "Okay, but if shit goes sideways, you're on the phone to me and I'm coming to get you, got it?"

I nodded, then gave him a hug. "Don't tell Dean until we're gone, okay? There's no way he'll see reason about this."

"Is that what I'm doing?"

I choked on a laugh. "Let's be honest, you're the calm one when it comes to you two."

"I don't feel so calm right now," he replied, opening the bathroom door to reveal a rather pissed-off looking bear. How he'd gotten into the locked room, I had no idea. "I'll see you after tonight." It was a thinly veiled order, demanding I come home in one piece. Then he turned to the bear. "You make sure of that."

Then he walked across my room and out the door.

WE ALL CONGREGATED outside at the designated time: Foust, Brunton, Jagger, Knox, Kat, Grizz, and me, to be exact.

"Shotgun!" Kat shouted as she darted toward the vehicles. Jagger just shook his head as he followed her.

"It's cool," I yelled after them. "I'll ride bitch, wedged between the bear and the ginger. No problem." I looked over at Grizz and jerked my head toward the car. "Go make some room for me, would ya?"

"Piper?" Knox called as Grizz strolled toward the vehicle. "You ready?"

"Yep! Let's find this bastard and shake him down."

Knox looked at me like I had three heads. "We're not trying to get money from him..."

"Oh, you know what I mean!" I argued, slapping his stomach as I walked by.

"What the fuck is taking you so long?" Kat shouted from the passenger door of the car.

For the sake of expedience, we ran to the SUV. I managed to get into the middle row after Grizz threw Brunton over the back of the seat. Jagger put his hands up in surrender and climbed over of his own free will. Smart wolf.

Once we were driving through the city, Jagger and Knox worked to pin down where Mack would most likely be inside the underground gambling club. It wasn't too far from the building that housed the Faerie portal in Chinatown; from what I gathered, it sounded like he ran a lot of his operations from there. Another shady supernatural in my life—just what I needed.

"So what's the plan?" Kat asked, looking over at Knox. When he didn't immediately answer, she needled at him. "You do have a plan, right? Because waltzing into a place like that seems like a suicide mission."

"Same plan as before. Brunton's going in to draw him out. Then we get our answers."

Kat laughed. "That would be an amazing plan if the goal was to get him thrown out or killed in under five minutes."

"Do you have something you'd like to share with us, Kat?" Knox replied, sounding every bit as annoyed as he felt.

"I might," she said with a shrug. Then she turned in her seat to look back at the rest of us. "Jagger! You said Mack is a sketchy motherfucker, right?"

"The sketchiest. He's into all kinds of illegal shit."

"Does he have a weakness for the ladies?"

"Weakness? No. But he loves to work them over—uses shit against them to make them do what he wants."

The mischief in Kat's smile was unmistakable. "I'm guessing he's well protected in a place like this?"

"Yeah," Jagger said, leaning forward to rest his arms on the back of my seat. "He never went anywhere without about a dozen of us."

"I know how I can draw him out—get him alone long enough to get what we need," she said.

"How do you plan to do that?" Knox asked, daring a glance in her direction.

"Simple," she explained, cupping her breasts over her shirt. "With these."

"Yeah, Kat... I don't know about that," Jagger said, concern in his voice.

"Relax. I'll let him think he's going to get what he wants and then shut him the fuck down. Wouldn't be the first time I've had to play that card."

Knox growled, looking over at her while we idled at a red light. "With us, you don't have to play that card ever again."

I expected Kat to fluff over his sentiment, but the intensity and sincerity in his voice seemed to affect her as much as it did me. The thought of using her as sexual bait to draw out Mack was repugnant to him. Whether she was pack or not, Knox still saw her as his to protect. Kat's lingering silence spoke volumes.

Then she found her voice. "I don't have to do anything. *Ever*," she replied, setting him straight. "But if I choose to do something, it's because I want to. This fucker sold us all out, not just your boy back there. For that he's going down, and if I have to dangle my little kitty cat in front of him to make that happen, I'll do it. For *all* of us."

"Kat..." I started before she cut me off.

"That's the plan and that's final." She looked over her shoulder at me. "It's going to be fine, Piper."

Another rumble echoed through the vehicle, but this time it wasn't Knox.

Grizz leaned forward and put his hand on Kat's shoulder, demanding her attention.

"You want to come in with me, big guy? I don't think that'll help with the whole seduction thing, unless Mack swings both ways..."

"Nope. Definitely not," Jagger interrupted.

"But Grizz and I could go in with you," I said, the idea coming to me in a flash. "The werewolves in this city won't know us. And if they recognize you, Kat, it won't matter." I managed to cut myself off before I said why, but she knew as well as I did that she was well known in the supernatural community. News of Jensen's death and Kat's widow status would be widely known by now. Even those that didn't know her personally would have heard of the lone female wolf and her personal tragedy.

Kat gave me a look of understanding that chilled me to the bone. She not only knew that was true; she planned to use that fact as leverage to get Mack alone.

"I hope they do," she said, turning back around. "I'm banking on it."

Silence fell upon the vehicle and it remained until we reached the block the gambling club's building was on. Kat jumped out without another word, then threw her jacket back in and slammed the door. She waited outside the vehicle for Grizz and me with her back to us, casing the building.

"Piper, you cannot let her out of your sight, understand?" Knox said, looking at me in the rearview mirror. I nodded. "The second she gets him alone, you send me a message. We'll be there."

"Try to get him into the back alley," Jagger added. "That's where he always used to go when he was going to...you know..."

"Fuck someone?" Brunton said. His reply sounded crude, but I knew him well enough to know that under his brusque tone lay a note of concern. It seemed like he didn't like Kat's plan any more than the rest of us.

I opened my mouth to speak, but Kat's fist banging on the door cut me off.

"Let's go already," she said before starting down the narrow way between the buildings that led to the entrance tucked away behind them.

"Coming!" I shouted before looking at Grizz. "We've got this, right?"

He nodded once, then set intense eyes on the werewolf heading into the lion's den. With that confirmation, I opened the door and hopped out, Grizz right behind me. I checked my phone to make sure it was on and charged and ready to message Knox the second we needed him. But doubt niggled at the back of my mind. Anyone in direct service to fey royalty was an enemy that couldn't be underestimated.

And I wondered if we were doing just that.

19

We made our way to the sketchy looking entrance, complete with security at the door. That made me wonder if we were heading into a mixed establishment. If so, shit was about to get a lot more complicated.

Kat strode up to him and stuck her chest out, putting the girls right out there on display. The bouncer, not immune to the power of her tits, dropped his gaze and leered.

"I need to make a little money," Kat said, unflinching. "Care to let a girl in there so she can make a living?"

"You could make it another way," he said, licking his lips.

"I don't know," she said, leaning toward him. "I'm pretty damn good at cards."

He considered her for a second before jerking his head toward the door. She strutted past him, and I followed her until a massive arm slammed down in front of me, blocking me.

"Not you."

Grizz growled behind me, and I reached back and put my hand on his leg.

"We're with her."

"Not tonight you're not."

I looked past him at Kat, who shook her head no before she kept on toward the building.

So not the plan.

"Listen," I said, softening my voice. "She and I are..." I tried my best to give him a suggestive look, but he didn't seem to catch my meaning.

"You're what?"

"Well, we work *together*, if you know what I mean." I let my fingers trail down his arm lightly while I smiled up at him suggestively. Realization dawned on him and he laughed. It was a harsh, biting sound that rang out down the narrow corridor.

"Tell you what, you let me sample the goods and I'll let you in."

Before I could say a word, Grizz's hand shot out over my head and grabbed the bouncer's neck. He lifted him up so high that the guy's shins were dangling in my face.

"I don't think my bodyguard cares for you plan," I said without a hint of my previous flirtation. "Want to rethink letting me in?"

"Go," he said, his voice strained against Grizz's hold.

"Great idea!" Grizz tossed the man aside and put his hand on the small of my back to usher me in. "See you later."

We entered the main door, which led to a set of stairs that led down. Of course his underground gambling club was literally underground. Why wouldn't it be?

After two flights into his subterranean den of sin, we walked through an opening that exposed the entire estab- lishment. A vast room with card tables and sofas and bars stretched out for yards. It was surprisingly large. My eyes immediately started scanning the room for Kat.

Grizz spotted her before I did and took my hand in his to drag me through the packed house. He bulldozed through patrons like they didn't matter; all he cared about was getting to Kat before she disappeared. When I finally spotted her, she was lounging next to the bar, talking to a plain-looking middle-aged man. I couldn't tell if he was Mack, or even a supernatural, so I knew we had to get closer. Grizz seemed to share my thought and made a beeline for the bar. He all but shoved some poor sap aside so we could cozy up to the bar right next to Kat and her new friend. Eavesdropping in a place that loud would prove challenging, but I positioned myself as close to her as I could and hoped for the best.

"So you're all alone now?" the guy said to her. I saw him lean in closer out of my periphery. My heart thumped wildly in my chest.

"For now."

"Why are you here? Looking to make some connections?"

"I'm looking to make some money, but connections are always good. I lost most of mine when Jensen died. The vampires tossed me out before his ashes had a chance to cool."

A pause.

"Heartless fucks. We should kill them all."

"I've thought about it," she replied before taking a sip of her drink. "All in good time though."

"You in the market to join a pack?" he asked, sounding particularly interested in her answer.

"I'm looking to survive at the moment, Kent. That's all."

Another wolf, but not Mack. I let out the breath I'd been holding and took a big swig of the drink I'd ordered.

"You know..." he started, clearly thinking things through as he spoke. "My buddy Mack is always looking for new wolves with something to offer."

I didn't need to see Kent's face to know what 'something to offer' meant. I put my hand on Grizz's arm to keep him still. I could feel the tension rolling off him. The last thing we needed was for him to start a fight in a club full of supernaturals. We'd already done that once. It hadn't gone so smoothly.

"I've got lots to offer," Kat replied, leaning her back against the bar. "Where's this Mack? I'd need to talk to him first. The vampires have given me trust issues. I'm sure you understand."

Kent threw back the rest of his drink before slamming the glass down on the bar.

"Pretty sure I can find him. Wait here. I'll be back in a minute."

Kat raised her glass to him then turned to face the bar, leaning on her elbows. Her arm brushed up against mine and I looked over at her.

"Hi," I said casually, as though I didn't know her.

"Hey." She took another swig of her drink. "Got a phone I can borrow?"

I pulled it out and shot her a look that said 'what the fuck are you doing?' She smirked at me, then took the phone from my hand. Her thumbs flew across the screen, typing something before handing it back to me.

"Thanks."

"Important text?" I asked.

"Just telling a friend when and where to meet me. I think I'll be leaving here sooner than I expected."

Before I could reply, an arm reached between us, clamping down on the bar. Kat and I both turned to find a rugged looking man smiling at us. He was large and intimidating, both in size and presence, and his dark hazel eyes seemed to take in everything around him. He pushed his dark brown hair from his face and smiled.

"Sorry sweetheart," he said to me. "Not interested in you. At least not yet." His gaze then fell upon Kat, who'd spun around in the cage of his arms to face him. And to put her girls on display yet again. Even fully clothed, Kat exuded sex, trying to or not.

But especially when she tried.

"You're going to hurt the poor girl's feelings," she said, feigning sympathy.

He merely shrugged in response.

He looked at me one more time, the devil in his eyes. He stared until I turned around, having been dismissed. Kat's plan was starting to make me really nervous. Mack was scarier than I'd imagined.

"So you're the wolf that mated the enforcer," he said, curiosity in his voice. "Something wrong with your own kind? Got a thing against male wolves?"

"Nope. I've got a thing against small cocks. Jensen won the big dick award. And let's face it, if you're looking for someone powerful, the enforcers are an impressive crowd. They practically have a free pass in this city."

"You like to break the rules?" he asked, leaning closer to Kat.

"I like to do what I want," she replied. "Jensen let me."

"Feisty," Mack replied, pressing his body against hers. "I like feisty."

Kat reached down between them and grabbed his package.

"Where were you when I was looking for a mate?" she asked, heat so thick in her voice that I nearly combusted.

Then Mack laughed and it sent a chill down my spine.

"You get right to the point, don't you?" he asked. I could see his hand running up her side toward her breast, and I had to quell every urge to jump up and tell him to leave her the fuck alone. She'd known this would happen. She was taking one for the team.

Right before he reached his destination, her hand shot up and caught his, stopping him short.

"Feisty, remember?" she said, staring at him. "You have to pay to play, my friend."

"What's the price?" he asked, his lips brushing against her neck. How she wasn't cringing was beyond me.

"*Refuge.*"

He pulled away.

"You want to join the pack?"

"This city's gone to shit," she said with a shrug. "Can you blame me?"

"No," he replied, amusement in his tone. "I can't, but now you see, you just gave away your leverage in this situation. Perhaps you aren't as feisty as I thought."

"I'm cutting through the shit to get what I want," she argued.

"Your impatience is going to cost you now."

"Maybe," she said casually. "Or maybe I'm just letting you think you have the upper hand. Maybe this is exactly what I wanted."

"We'll see about that," he said, taking her arm to lead her toward the back of the room. I couldn't see a set of stairs anywhere. No marked exits in sight. Wherever they were headed, it didn't look like the back alley.

"Watch where they go," I said to Grizz as I whipped my

phone out. I pulled up my text messages and found the one Kat had sent to Knox: "See you in five…"

I hit call and held the phone to my ear while I struggled to see where Mack was leading Kat. The crowd seemed to swallow them whole.

"Shit!" I muttered to myself. "Grizz, follow her. I'm going to go get the boys." The bear shook his head just as Knox answered. "Goddammit! I don't have time for your shenanigans."

"What's going on?"

"Mack is taking Kat somewhere not mentioned in the playbook. You need to get down here now." While Knox barked orders at the guys, I grabbed Grizz by the shirt collar and pulled his face near mine. "Find her!"

I jumped off my seat, phone in hand, and tried to push my way through the gambling mob to little effect. Grizz blew past me, tossing bodies out of his way. It wasn't subtle, but it was damn effective.

"We're coming down the stairs now," Knox said. I could hear the echo of footsteps on the other end. Knowing the cavalry was coming made my chest relax a tiny bit. Unleashing my powers in a mixed environment was a last-resort option only. What I needed was more brute force, and Knox and the boys had that in spades.

Grizz picked up speed as we neared the far side of the room. Once we met the brick wall, he yanked me to the left, headed toward a tight hallway. And it was empty.

"Did they go down here?" I asked. He didn't bother trying to reply. His increased pace was answer enough. "Grizz… tell me you didn't lose her."

A growl. A cloud of mortar dust.

Grizz stopped short and I slammed into his back.

"Where are you?" Knox shouted at me over the phone as though he'd asked me more than once.

"Go to the back wall. There's a small hallway on the left side."

At the end of the narrow way was a utility closet of sorts —an old-fashioned broom closet. It wasn't big enough to be used as an actual door, but I wondered...

"The door," I said aloud as I squeezed past Grizz to reach it. As I neared it, a familiar rush of magic washed over me. I ran to it and grabbed the handle, throwing it open. Behind it was a brick wall. A door to nowhere.

Or was it?

I reached my hand out and was met with a strange sort of resistance—one that was decidedly not brick.

"Motherfucker!" I shouted, throwing my phone aside. "He took her to Faerie, Grizz!" The look on his face was murderous. For a moment, I contemplated whether or not we should go. But the thought of Mack's hands on Kat made my skin crawl, and before I knew it, I was dragging Grizz through the veil with me. If anything happened to her because I hadn't had her back, I'd never forgive myself.

Neither would Grizz.

We were spit out in the middle of a vast, open field. Tall grass surrounded us, but nothing else. It seemed to stretch on for miles, the terrain flatter than the plains states I'd driven through when I escaped NYC. I spun to search for her in every direction, calling her name repeatedly to no avail. Even though their head start had been short, they were somehow long gone.

Fucking screwy fey time.

I tried calling my powers to search for her, but unlike in the earthly realm, nothing happened.

"Dammit!" I shouted, Grizz pinning concerned eyes on

me. "We have to go back. I can't search for her here." My rising panic threatened to undo me right then, but I forced myself to keep it together for Kat's sake. The girl could hold her own any day of the week, but Mack was an unknown—a wild card—and the fact that he had a fey portal in his establishment didn't bode well at all. I feared Kat might be outmatched.

Then I feared for what that could mean.

I reached out into the air around me, trying to home in on the portal. It didn't take long to find it, and I snatched Grizz's hand again and dragged him through it with me. It spat us out into the hallway, tossing me right into Knox. I practically knocked him over with the force, but Jagger steadied him.

Apparently fey time was screwier than I thought.

"He took her to Faerie," I blurted out. "I can't find her there, Knox. I can't search for her like I can here, and they were nowhere to be seen... what do we do? We can't lose her..."

"We won't," he said, bending down to level his gaze with mine. "Listen to me. I need you to calm down and focus. Can you do that?" I took a deep breath and tried to center myself. When I nodded, he continued. "We need to go outside and see if we can track her. There are fey portals all around this city. They may have slipped in one and out another. That could be why you didn't see them."

"Then let's go!" I shouted, shoving him back down the hall. We ran in single file until we broke out into the main room. Knox, Foust, Brunton, and Jagger cut a path through the room like missiles while Grizz prodded me on from the rear of the pack. Our exit was a bit of a blur. My mind was consumed by dark thoughts, all of which involved unfortunate fates for Kat. I tried to remember that she was resourceful and tough as nails, but those truths did little to assuage the what-ifs taking over.

When we emerged into the cool evening air, dusk settling in around the city, I looked up at the darkening sky and closed my eyes.

"Take me to Kat," I said, my voice low but commanding. I added a "quickly" to it just to be sure.

The wind that had guided me so many times before rustled my hair, tossing it wildly in front of me. I sprinted down the corridor without another thought. The boys all trailed me until we approached the car. The wind died the second we ran alongside the SUV. My bewilderment didn't last long.

"Get in!" I shouted, throwing open the passenger door. The boys didn't question my order. They jumped into the vehicle and slammed the doors, ready to chase down the sketchy bastard that had kidnapped our girl.

For a moment, nothing happened. Our guide had abandoned us. But then small droplets of rain began to fall from a cloudless sky onto the windshield. It drew away, headed east. Knox threw the SUV in gear and pulled out, winding his way through traffic to follow our private storm.

I watched the clock, begging it to slow down. If we'd lost much time in Faerie, that meant Mack had had more time to carry out whatever ominous plan he had for Kat.

"This is taking too long!" I shouted before punching the dash.

"Piper," Knox said, doing his best to sound calm, as though I couldn't see his hands white-knuckling the steering wheel in my periphery. "We're going to find her."

"You didn't see how he looked at her, Knox." I literally shuddered at the way his greedy eyes had sized her up.

"And she'll probably take his arm off if he tries to touch her."

"Something isn't right about him," I replied, shaking my head.

"He's a werewolf," Jagger said. "Just like Kat."

I wheeled on him in my seat. "He *was*, whenever it was that you last knew him, but how long ago was that? A year? Five?" Jagger just stared at me silently and my anger grew. "You have no fucking clue what he is now or what he's capable of. He's an alpha, and Kat made him think she was willing to do anything to join his pack." I let my words sink in for a second. "And I mean *anything*, Jagger."

"Alpha or not," Brunton said, his expression hard and unreadable, "she's hard as fuck to bring down. He'd better have a small army waiting for him, or he's in trouble."

"Which he very well might have, wherever he is."

Jagger looked out the window to see where we were. His eyes were strained, like he was trying to figure something out. Like he recognized where we were.

"Knox..."

"What, Jagger?"

"Mack used to live around here. A couple blocks up."

I looked over at Knox, who hazarded a glance at me.

"Drive faster," I said, and Knox complied, damn near flooring it through traffic. He wove the beast of a vehicle through the cars like it was an Indy race car. The storm got stronger as we neared our destination, raining on everyone around us. I looked up at the sky as lightning shot down, hitting the lightning rod on top of a high-rise building.

"There!" I screamed, pointing at it.

"That's the one!" Jagger shouted.

"Motherfucker has a portal to Faerie in his apartment,"

Brunton said under his breath. And there was nothing friendly about the way he said it.

Knox pulled up outside the building and double-parked the SUV, much to the chagrin of the doorman. He chucked the keys at the poor man before slamming through the entrance. We all followed behind him, ignoring the threats from the gentleman about calling the cops.

"Shut him up," I said under my breath. I heard the thump of a body hitting the pavement and looked back to see him passed out in front of the building.

We filed into the elevator and pushed the 'close door' button until it finally obeyed. Then we stood there and stared at the numbers on the display. I held my finger out in front of them and closed my eyes.

"Show me which one," I said. A gust of air from the vent knocked me forward, forcing me to hit the PH button.

"That's new," Jagger said from behind me.

The ride up to the top floor was agonizing. Every passing second made me want to jump out of my skin. By the time the elevator came to a stop, I was ready to punch through the metal doors to get to Kat.

I was the first out of the elevator, closing the distance between it and the penthouse door in a few strides. I could hear signs of a struggle inside. Mack was shouting horrible things at Kat, but I heard nothing in response. Before I could contemplate what that meant, Knox's foot flew past me toward the door, busting it down in a seamless move.

We all raced into the apartment poised for a fight—then caught a glimpse of the one already taking place. The expansive living room before us had been practically laid to waste. Kat stood on the far side of the only unbroken table smiling wickedly at Mack, who was getting up from having been knocked down.

"Hey guys," she said casually as blood streamed down her face. "This is my new friend Mack. We're just taking some time to get to know each other a little better. If you want to come back in maybe five minutes, I think we'll be fully acquainted."

"Kat..."

"It's cool, Piper. I've got this."

Mack appeared totally unfazed by our presence. Instead, he glared across the room at Kat, his golden eyes burning with rage. His face was bloodied, though not as badly as Kat's, and his arm was bent at a strange angle. Then I noticed the bone protruding through his jacket.

He sprang halfway across the room to get her, but he was intercepted along the way. Knox tackled him to the ground in a graceful move and held him there with a knee in his back.

"Sorry to cut in on your date like this," Knox said, looking up to Kat. "But I think it's late. Time to get you home."

Kat licked the blood from her lip and feigned a pout.

"But I was just starting to like him." She walked around the table to where Knox held Mack captive. "He's much more fun to be around when he's bleeding."

"You're going to die bitch!" Mack snarled.

Kat buried her foot in his face in response.

"You had your chance to kill me and you blew it," she said, sounding bored. "Don't call me names because you're bitter."

Knox hauled Mack up to his feet and slammed him down in a busted up wingback chair. He made a move to get up, but Brunton was there with his hands on Mack's shoulders, shoving him back down. His claws were extended and digging into the alpha's flesh for good measure.

"Piper," Knox said, looking over to me. "Search the place for a portal."

I closed my eyes and waited for the pull of magic to call to me. It didn't take long before it did. From an abstract painting on the left wall of the living room I could feel the call of Faerie.

"There," I said, pointing to it.

"Good job. Now, do me a favor and shut it down."

I walked over to the massive canvas hanging on the wall and ran my hand across the front of it to take in the breadth of the opening. It was much larger than the one in the broom closet we'd entered earlier that night. Grizz growled when my hand got too close to the surface, and he actually yanked me back one time when I skimmed the rough fabric.

"It's okay, buddy," I said, giving his arm a squeeze. "I've done it before. I can do it again."

"Don't!" Mack shouted from behind me, followed by the distinct sound of fist meeting face.

"You talk when I say you can talk," Knox warned, cocking his arm back for another blow. Kat caught it, pushing her way between the alphas.

"If you'd be so kind as to allow me the honor. I wasn't quite finished with him when you and the cavalry arrived."

Her sharp blue eyes held an undercurrent of need as they stared up at Knox. After a moment he relented, letting her stand before Mack, a sadistic grin overtaking her face.

"I told you there would be a price to pay for touching me," she said casually, looking down at her hand as though she'd broken a nail. But she clearly hadn't. Instead, she flicked at one of her claws that had extended. Bending down slowly to put her face in Mack's, she placed the blade-like claw at his neck, pressing it in until a single drop of blood escaped. "The last person that tried to without my consent didn't fare so well."

The claw dug in deeper.

"Kat," Knox said, his tone cautionary.

"I know," she replied, pulling back a bit. "We need him to help find our little admirer." Then, in a blur of movement, Kat's clawed hand swiped down at Mack's lap. "But he doesn't need that to do it." The delayed scream Mack let out was half human, half howl, and wholly terrifying. Every hair on my body stood on end. "He's all yours," she said, turning to stroll toward me. Blood spurted behind her, creating a rainbow of red framing her approach. For the first time in my life, I feared what Kat was capable of. Seeing the look of distress on my face, Kat simply smiled. "He'll heal, don't worry. It's just a flesh wound."

"Piper..." Knox called, assessing the injury. "A little help over here?"

I muttered under my breath for Mack to be healed and waited for the downpour of blood to cease. When it did, Kat looked annoyed.

"You couldn't have let him come a little closer to dying before saving him?" She shrugged at my lack of response, then came to stand beside me. "I wonder how long it's going to take to get anything useful out of him."

Mack was a lowlife on the grandest scale—Jagger had made that point clear. His moral compass hadn't seen due north in a long time. I wondered just how deep he was in with both the fey king and queen, and how hard it would be to get anything useful out of him about the assassin.

"Let's get something clear before we get started here," Knox said, drawing my attention to the interrogation behind us. "Jagger is dead to you. Your beef with him is over, understood?"

"Like I give a shit about that pussy."

Knox's fist met Mack's face for the second time that night. "*Understood*?"

"Yeah," Mack said, spitting a mouthful of blood over the arm of the chair. "I got it."

"Good. Now you're going to explain your connection to the fey royals."

"I don't have one."

"You have a fucking portal in your home," Knox shouted, craning Mack's head to where Kat, Grizz, and I stood. "The queen doesn't hand those out like party favors. Pretty sure the king doesn't either."

"I bought that painting at an auction. I had no fucking clue there was a portal attached to it."

"Oh for fuck's sake," Kat sighed. "Just let me slice his dick all the way off this time. He'll tell you whatever you want to know if he thinks Piper might reattach it for him."

"And you just happen to have another portal at your club?" Knox continued, ignoring Kat's outburst.

Mack shrugged.

"She gave you that portal."

"No."

"*Lie.*"

A sharp sound rang out through the penthouse from beside me. I looked over to see Kat admiring her claws yet again.

"I'll let her do it," Knox said, leaning in closer to Mack. "I'll let her have full retribution for whatever you did or threatened to do to her. Then we'll destroy your portal and burn your club to the ground. The queen doesn't take kindly to someone treating her gifts so disrespectfully. It would only be a matter of time before she came for you... maybe the king too." To Mack's credit, he held firm against Knox's interrogation, not saying a word. Knox looked over at me and gave a slow nod. I called for the blue fire I had so many times before. Mack's eyes went wide as it danced around my wrist until I flicked it at the portal.

"Destroy it," I said under my breath.

I watched as the fabric turned to ash and floated around Grizz and Kat as it blew away, leaving behind a tiny ripple in the ether. A crack in the veil between Faerie and Earth. My fingers reached for it, tracing its contours and sealing it closed with a white-blue light so bright I had to turn away from it and trust my magic to weld it shut.

Mack looked at me with wide eyes. It was like he was seeing me for the first time. Recognizing that I was a big player in the game.

"You..." he said, his voice distant.

"Yep, me. The one that bested the queen of the fey and kept you from screwing Jagger over with a life of servitude to that psycho bitch." I walked toward him, passing Jagger and Foust along the way. Neither attempted to stop me. "I can shut the fey queen down, so don't think it'll take much for me to rain torture down on you if you dick around. And if you touched Kat...." I sucked in a breath between my teeth. "Then you and I are really going to have a problem on our hands."

"You're the one with a problem," he said, smiling up at me like he wasn't already beaten. Like the game wasn't over.

"The king's little puppet? He's going to meet his end pretty soon. And you're going to help make that happen because you're going to tell me everything you know about him, starting with why he's attacking Knox's pack."

Mack laughed. It was a small chuckle at first, but it grew and grew until the booming tenor of it filled the room. "If you haven't figured out the why, you are the dumbest fucking lot ever."

Blue flame erupted out of my palms, which I extended toward his face. I stopped only inches away, and he winced. Not so tough in the face of a fiery death.

"Maybe I can burn it out of you," I whispered, leaning in closer to him. I let the flames lick at his face, the sizzle of flesh echoing through the room, followed closely by his screams. When the fire relented, he was far more talkative.

"He's after Knox."

"We figured that much. We want to know why."

"I don't know anything beyond that," Mack said, still staring at the blue flames licking at his face.

"Truth," Knox growled. "How do we find the assassin?"

"No clue. He comes when he's sent."

Another growl. Knox looked over at me, demanding my attention. The grim realization he'd come to was clear in his eyes.

"He's watching us somehow," he said. His blue eyes began to glow yellow as he grew angrier.

"Spies," Foust suggested, looking around the room.

Mack let out a pained laugh. "There's a question you haven't asked me yet that's probably the most important one. It might explain a few things for you." Knox shot him a look that said 'talk now before my patience runs out'. "You don't ask *who* the assassin is."

Silence stretched out for a couple of seconds before Kat snapped.

"Then fucking tell us before I slice your dick off!"

Mack's eyes turned to her, full of hatred, then back to Knox.

"You know him," he said. "From what I understand, he's basically family..."

Knox's tight features went slack and he took a step back from Mack.

"Who is it?" Brunton demanded, stepping in front of Knox to rough Mack up.

"Liam..." Knox said, his voice low and empty, his skin as pale as a ghost.

"Who's Liam?" I asked, searching every face in the room for answers. Jagger looked as confused as Kat. But Foust, Brunton, and Knox—their expressions were all the same. Complete and utter disbelief.

"But he's dead," Foust finally said. "And even if he were alive, we would have known his scent."

"Maybe not... not if the king altered his being," Knox said, the pain in his eyes visible from across the room. "What if we abandoned our brother to his fate?" The originals looked at one another. Silence. "Maybe we deserve what's happening to us..."

"Liam was the other original," Kat said, her tone flatter than I'd ever heard it. I shot her a look and she simply shrugged. "I overheard them talking about the king and Faerie the other night. They said there were four."

"So this is about payback," Brunton said.

Knox nodded. "He's hitting us where it hurts most."

"By attacking what's ours." Brunton held Knox's gaze until his eyes darted to Kat and back again. "He's making it personal."

"Which means he has to be watching us in order to know," Foust added.

As the three of them turned their attention to Mack, ready to bleed him until he gave up every morsel of information he had, I heard a call from somewhere behind me. It was soft and low and barely audible, but for whatever reason, I heard it over the din. Felt it, maybe. As though it was a call to my magic as much as it was to me.

I looked over my shoulder out of reflex. Nobody was there. But still, the echo of that call surrounded me, drawing me to the opposite side of the room from where the queen's portal had been. The more I moved toward the wall, the stronger the whisper grew.

Piper...

The others in the room seemed unfazed by the voice, all of them circling Mack and shouting. Even Grizz was in on the action. But I didn't care—I just kept inching away from them toward my name. It wrapped around me, coaxing me. When I bumped into the wall, I turned to find a strange bronze figurine of sorts hanging right before my eyes. It practically begged to be touched.

"So beautiful..." I muttered to myself as my finger grazed the bottom edge of what appeared to be a face. The longer I stared at it, the more into focus it came, revealing beauty that my mind could not comprehend. A dark and ominous masculinity that both thrilled and terrified me.

I leaned closer to it.

"Just one kiss," I said to myself before my lips grazed soft, warm flesh that kissed me back.

"I'm glad you could come," the voice said. "I've been waiting for you..."

I opened my eyes to see a wickedly handsome being staring at me, his piercing blue eyes assessing me through the stray blond hair that had fallen in his face. I reached out to touch the sharp angles of his jaw and cheeks, but he caught my hand and pressed it to his perfect lips.

"I'm sorry," I said, apologizing for making him wait. I hated myself for inconveniencing him in any way.

"We need to talk," he said, stepping back from me. The

distance between us made my chest hurt more than it ever had. I couldn't stand being apart from him. "You and I—we have a common interest. A mutual enemy."

"Who?" I asked, my voice thin and wavering.

He cocked his head at me, curiosity in his eyes. "My wife."

He took another step back from me, and I felt my body lurch forward, reaching for him.

"I will kill her," I replied. I sounded wild and feral, ready to shred her body to bits just to have him all to myself. He laughed at my response, the warm tenor of his voice caressing me in places it should not have.

"It won't be that easy," he said, coming closer. "But I will give you something in return. Something you desire."

"You?" I asked, reaching for his face.

"Peace," he said, stroking my cheek. "You do know that you cannot have them both, don't you? They will never concede to that." He circled behind me, his fingertips dancing along my jaw and down my neck. My breath caught in my throat, the trail of burning they left in their wake an exquisite torture. "But what if there were another option?" he mused, stopping behind me. "One that could give you everything they had to offer without the sacrifice? Without the pain and indecision you clearly suffer from?" He pressed closer to me, his chest grazing my back, his lips at my ear. "What if there were a door number three?" His whispers sent chills up my spine. "I wonder, Piper... do you like pain? Is that why you are unwilling to let them go?" He traced the lobe of my ear with his nose. "I could give you pain..."

Just as my body began to sink into his, I felt it jerked away like a dog on a leash. I struggled against the force, already missing his touch. I looked back at him for aid, but he simply smiled.

"I will send for you soon, Piper. Tell Knox I said hello..."
Then he disappeared.

I fell back onto the floor of Mack's penthouse and looked up at a circle of faces staring down at me. It took my mind a second to realize who they were—where I was. Once I did, my body started to shake.

"What... what just happened?"

Grizz reached down and picked me up, setting me on my feet in the center of the group.

"That's what we want to know," Kat said, her anger belying the fear she felt. I could see in her wild stare that she was freaked out by whatever had just gone down.

"I... I don't know. One second, you guys were grilling Mack, and the next, I heard my name and I walked over to the wall." I looked over to where I'd been when things started to get fuzzy with my recollection of events. A strange looking bronze figurehead hung there, and the second my eyes fell upon it, my body went cold. "That... what is that?"

"A portal," Knox said, his voice grim. His expression was even more ominous. A mix of anger and fear furrowed his brow and tensed his jaw. Whatever had happened while I was off trying to throw myself at the beautiful creature must have been bad. Really bad.

"To where?" I asked, though I didn't really need to. As the haze lifted from my mind, I realized where I'd gone because I knew whom I'd met. The fey king had beckoned me to his land—tricked me into coming to him—and I'd fallen for it. Just as I'd fallen for him. I shuddered at the power of his magic, rooted in control. Knox's desire to escape from his ownership made even more sense in that moment.

"The fey king's side of Faerie."

"How did you get me out?" I asked, the logistics unclear.

"Well," Kat said, "since you were literally halfway through it before someone saw you, I dove for your legs. I managed to keep you in place, but when Knox got over there and tried to yank you back, you fell farther in. If Grizz hadn't been here to anchor you, I think you might have found yourself at home with the fey king."

"I think I almost did that myself," I mumbled. Knox's eyes narrowed, and I let out a sigh. "There's something about him—I wanted to be there. I fought to stay with him."

"That is one of his gifts on his side of the veil," Foust said, his tone apologetic. "It's not your fault, Piper. You can see now why we required the fey queen's assistance to escape him."

Boy could I ever.

"What did he want?" Knox asked, stepping closer to me. The tight fold of his arms across his chest made my heart sink. He was scared to touch me—or too disgusted to.

"He wants me to help him kill the fey queen."

"I like him already," Kat said to herself.

"He said he'd give me something I desired if I did."

Knox let out a mirthless laugh. "That bastard. That's why he's picking us off. It's not to get back at me—to get me to return. It's to leverage your love of the pack to force you into doing his bidding."

"Smart," Brunton said with a growl.

"And sneaky as fuck," Foust added. "Exactly his style."

"Sending one of our own after us," Knox started before cutting himself off. "I cannot imagine what he's done to him in our absence. How he's twisted what we did to change him."

"Not to mention how he's jacked him up magically," Brunton said. "Liam was like us, but whatever he is now, it ain't one of us anymore."

"He'll keep sending him, won't he? Until he gets what he wants?" I asked. Knox, Foust, and Brunton all nodded in unison. "Shit... shit! What are we going to do? He said he'd come for me soon... but how? Do you think he'll send Liam for me?" Grizz's growl echoed through the penthouse. I reached back and took his hand in mine. "I know, buddy, but you don't understand what he's like. What he's capable of."

"Question," Kat said, walking over to the back of the couch. She casually hitched her hip onto it, then continued. "How come you didn't use your magic on him? I mean, it worked pretty damn well on the fey queen when we were there."

Mother. Fucker.

"I don't know," I said, which was true enough. Kind of. "I didn't feel like I wanted to." Because what I'd felt like doing was jumping his bones.

"If he caught her off guard, that could be reason enough," Knox said in my defense. "His thrall is unlike anything I've ever felt. If he chooses to turn it upon you, it is impossible to withstand. Or nearly impossible—I wouldn't count Piper out just yet."

When the group grew silent, each of us contemplating this new revelation, I realized something.

"Where's Mack?" I asked, pushing through the crowd to see if he was still there.

Brunton started laughing.

"Gone..."

I looked to Foust, who simply shrugged, and then to Knox.

"I had Dean come and take him. I believe he is incarcerated somewhere at the mansion—just in case we should need his services at some point."

"I wanted to kill him," Kat said, "but it seems I was outvoted this time."

I choked on a laugh.

"Since when do you yield to the voice of democracy?"

The smile she gave me in return was positively devilish. "Who said I planned to yield forever? The boys can think they're in control—for now." She pushed off the couch and walked toward the door. "Time to leave. This place reeks of new power and money—not my scene."

"Yeah. Let's go," I said. But I couldn't make myself move. I stood rooted in place as I stared at the bronze on the wall. I felt like it was watching me—like the fey king stood just beyond the shadows of the veil. With careful steps I walked toward it, summoning my magic. When I reached it, I called it all forth, the blue flame more brilliant than it had been since I'd healed the amulet. Then I watched as the bronze began to melt.

I thought I heard my name over the roar of the fire.

Once the portal was closed, I turned and headed toward the others hovering nearby. Together we left Mack's penthouse with more than we'd bargained for. The assassin was the fourth original werewolf, and the fey king was using him to leverage me into killing his wife. And though I wanted nothing more than to off the queen for all that she'd done to me and my family before me, I couldn't help but feel like there was a catch. One I wouldn't like. If we couldn't figure out what it was, and fast, I feared death would continue to stalk the wolves.

And I would yet again be the puppet in someone else's deadly game.

20

D rake was waiting for us in the front yard when we arrived home.

The lot of us filed into the mansion, where the rest awaited us. From the solemn looks on our faces, they could tell something was wrong. Especially the wolves. Merc met me at the top of the stairs and hugged me. He leaned in close and smelled my hair, then pushed me away, true and definite fear in his eyes.

"Where have you been?" he asked like an angry parent who was scared for his child.

"Do you want the long or short version?"

"I think everyone needs to hear this," Knox said, climbing the stairs toward us. He passed us by without so much as a backward glance, then made his way toward the media room, his pack following.

It wasn't long before the room was packed full of virtually everyone who resided in the mansion. Drake too. Once those of us that had sought Mack out that night explained how everything had gone down—including my impromptu half-trip to the fey king's realm—the shit hit the fan.

Merc and Knox were in a full-blown standoff, with me, once again, caught in the middle.

"How could you let that happen?" Merc growled, his control waning.

"I didn't 'let' anything happen. One second, she was standing there, and the next, her legs were dangling from the wall and disappearing fast. When I grabbed her, she slipped farther in. Grizz was the only one able to pull her back."

Merc shot the bear a look, and he puffed his chest in return.

"Liam is your problem to deal with from this point on," Merc declared, washing his hands of the pack.

"If you'll recall," Knox replied, "I never asked for your help. Piper volunteered hers of her own free will. Free will you seem happy to take from her."

Rage blossomed in Merc's dark stare, and I felt the vise in my chest clamp down on my lungs. I couldn't breathe. I could barely see. My legs felt numb and useless beneath me until they finally gave way. I would have crashed to the ground if it weren't for the strong arms that caught me. Pressed tight against a wall of chest, I felt a little strength return. My vision cleared and I found warm brown eyes staring down at me, so full of concern it was painful to look into them.

"I'm okay, Grizz. I just... it's just that..."

"You're stressed?" Kat suggested, her dry tone letting me know that she saw right through me. I looked around at all the prying eyes until I met Drake's studious gaze. He stormed toward me, knocking past Merc who stood partially in his path. He put his hand on my chest and closed his eyes. They flew open seconds later.

"It's fading," he said finally. Fear and sadness warred in his expression.

"What's fading?" Merc asked, the irritation in his tone plain.

Drake turned to face him, his body coiled with rage.

"Her magic."

The irritation fell from Merc's expression. "How?"

"*You*... you're how."

Knox stepped closer to Merc, a low growl escaping.

The two of them locked glares, and I thought the world would surely come to an end. They lunged at one another, and I collapsed in Grizz's arms.

"Enough!" Drake shouted. The command in his voice halted both Merc and Knox. The others just stood by and watched with blank expressions "Are you two so blind that you cannot see what's happening to her?" He stared at Knox and Merc, his anger flaring in his eyes. "You're killing her, and you're too wrapped up in hating one another to realize it. And she's too used to surviving on her own to see it either."

Grizz held me close, unwilling to put me down while Drake stepped forward, taking my place between the two males in my life. He was angry—angrier than I'd ever seen him before—and no amount of mental fatigue or stress or illness could blind me to it.

"Piper..." Knox started before Drake shut him down.

"No! You don't get to talk. You get to listen, before you fuck this up and she winds up dead. Because that *is* where she'll end up if you two can't rise above your petty war and acknowledge that which is so painfully obvious: she needs you *both*. The two of you represent something for her that she cannot find on her own—balance. Without one, she cannot survive the other."

"Well she sure as fuck isn't surviving both of them very well either," Dean chimed in, coming to stand next to Grizz. Jase joined him on the other side—always ready for a fight when it came to me.

"That's exactly my point, enforcer," Drake replied. "Because neither is willing to admit his shortcomings when it comes to her, they fight. And their fighting is forcing her back to a place in her mind where she survived without her magic, except that place no longer exists. Once you open Pandora's box, it can never be shut."

"What are you saying, Riddler?" Kat asked, leaning against the wall next to Jagger and the boys.

"I'm saying that her magic was suppressed for so long, and she survived because of that. But once she met him," Drake said, pointing at Knox, "everything changed. It was because of her connection to him and his wolves that she was able to do what she did to Kingston. Her full powers were released that night. If it hadn't been for her fear overriding them, she would have burned out." Drake then turned his attention to Merc, who stood silently before him. "You, on the other hand, stifle her magic when necessary—something she clearly needs—but too much of you cuts off the very power her being is connected to. The energy her soul thrives upon. Take that away from her and she fades."

I could see the grief in Merc's expression. He knew that his overbearingness was literally smothering me to death. He took a step away from me.

"Are you saying she's dying?" Kat asked, her voice suddenly thick with emotion. She'd only just lost her bloodbound, Jensen. Losing me would break her—I could practically feel her fear.

Drake's sympathetic gaze met mine and I knew it was true. Everything that I'd been trying to rationalize away finally made sense with his words. I was dying. The second I entertained that possibility, it became fact.

"How do we fix it?" I asked, trying to climb down out of Grizz's arms. They tightened around me in response. Apparently the bear wasn't ready to let go of me either—literally or metaphorically speaking.

"The three of you must all accept the hand you've been dealt," my mentor said, sounding truly remorseful. "This is your Achilles heel, Piper. Every powerful being has one. It is all that keeps them in check. You are forever dependent on others to keep your abilities under control because they are beyond you." He turned his gaze back toward Knox and Merc before letting his anger resurface. "So let me be clear on this matter. I don't care what kind of dysfunctional relationship dynamics you have to orchestrate, or whose ego might get trampled in the process. You need to figure it out because she won't be choosing either of you. She's not a prize to be won. She's a being beyond convention and has unconventional needs because of it. You either accept that or you don't. But if you don't, know that the consequence will be dire."

"She'll die," Knox growled as though that truth was an enemy he could rip apart. "Well I'm sure as fuck not going to let that happen." His angry eyes fell upon Merc, who stood stoically, staring at me.

"I cannot lose you," he said, his voice low and controlled. "Never again."

I wriggled in Grizz's hold, and he finally put me down gently, making sure I had my balance before I moved. I felt better already, the weight of my pending decision lifted in an instant. I did what I could to avoid thinking of the implications of Merc, Knox, and I forever being a triumvirate of sorts, but it wasn't something I could ignore indefinitely.

"How do you feel, Piper?" Drake asked as I took a step toward him.

"Better?"

He put his hand on my chest again, focusing on my thrum of magic. His steel grey eyes opened and peered into mine. A small smile tugged at his mouth.

"It is." He pulled his hand away and turned to stare at Merc and Knox. "And if these two can accept their positions, maybe it'll stay that way."

Grizz growled at them both and they acknowledged him, nodding once.

"They understand," I told him, patting his arm.

He walked around me and past Drake, cutting in front of Merc and Knox. He stopped for a second and lifted his fist in the air before opening it up, palm down, and walking away. By the time my sluggish mind registered the fact that Grizz had just dropped the mic on the two of them, he was already walking past the wolves, fist-bumping Jagger before taking up position next to him, leaning against the wall.

"The bear wins again," Kat laughed, slipping her arm around my shoulders. "Too bad he can't be your everything, Piper. He's so much more entertaining."

When tempers settled, the group disbanded. We were still no closer to a solution for Liam, but a weight had been lifted off of me, and most of the others as well. Knox and Merc's shaky truce had been taking a toll on everyone in the house—not just me. I hoped that, over time, we could do what Drake said and figure out a way to not only coexist, but work together to maintain my magic. Maybe even stop the fey king's pet.

21

I awoke from a tortured sleep.

The fey king's face was inescapable and I could almost feel his hands on me, coaxing me to him. And damned if my body didn't want to follow. Wiping the sweat from my face, I crept across the bedroom floor around Grizz and out of my room. I had no idea what time it was, but the mansion was quiet. Too quiet.

I took the butler's stairs down to the kitchen, hoping some tea might calm my mind. But when I heard two familiar voices coming from the dining room down the hall, I tiptoed toward them. Merc and Knox were arguing yet again, but this time there was less heat to it. Just frustration.

"That was not my doing," Merc said, maintaining an air of calm in the wake of whatever Knox had said, but I could hear the edges of his control fraying.

"Wasn't it?" Knox pressed. "If your blood bond runs so deep, then why couldn't you feel what you were doing to her? Why weren't you able to fight whatever it was that Kingston did to you?"

"He used that bond against me," Merc replied.

"You almost..." Knox cut himself off, trying to regain some measure of composure. While he did, Merc countered his argument.

I dared to move closer to the room.

"Would it be so different for you?" Merc asked. "If the fey king chose to use you as a weapon against Piper? Would that yield a different result?"

I heard Knox exhale hard. I crouched down low and hazarded a peek around the corner. He was pacing the room, his fingers entwined in his hair, pulling on it in frustration. He finally stopped, his back to both Merc and me. He braced his hands against the massive table and hung his head.

"You should have seen her," he started, all the heat and anger absent from his tone. "You should have seen her when I found her in the woods that day in Alaska—when she walked back up to her cabin to find me leaning against it. I could smell her fear from fifty yards away. She tried so hard to look unfazed by my presence, but knowing what I was had her so terrified she could barely talk. I knew right away that she was running from something."

"You just didn't expect that something to be me," Merc said, his tone flat and cold and full of remorse.

Knox shook his head, turning to face Merc. "The first night she came to meet the boys, Foust spooked her and she tried to run, but the second she flung the door open and looked out at the black of night, she froze. I had a feeling there was a vampire connection, but I kept that to myself. She was so skittish—I didn't want to drive her away."

"I'm thankful you didn't."

"Don't thank me yet," Knox replied, his expression hardening. "Because when I learned why she was running—that you had gone batshit crazy and tried to kill her—I vowed I'd end you if I ever saw you again." Merc's arms went wide, all but inviting Knox to try. "But I know you helped her heal me —kept her from burning out trying to save me and the boys. For that, I put that vow to rest."

"We have been at this impasse before, Knox."

Silence.

"Yeah. We have."

"It seems to be our curse."

"It seems it always will be."

More silence.

"Can you do it?" Merc asked. "Can you do what the warlock demands of us?"

"I can't afford to walk away, I know that much," Knox replied. "She needs me."

"She chose you out of necessity," Merc said.

Knox growled. "From what I've heard, the same could be said about you. That girl is a survivor. Every choice she ever made before her powers came to her was about survival. Including *you*. And now the cosmic joke is on us. She needs us *both*."

Merc had no response for that.

Before their conversation devolved, I slinked back down the hall on silent feet. I didn't stop until I reached my bedroom, grabbing the knob to enter. But the hairs on the back of my neck stood up, stopping me. A breeze blew past me, and I followed its path. I stared down the hallway, disbelief washing over me. I knew that I was seeing what I was seeing, but I still couldn't convince myself it wasn't a dream —or a nightmare.

"He wants to see you now," Liam said. His voice was low and sultry, and I wondered if it had always sounded that way or if he had been infused with the sexual draw of his maker. "He wants an answer."

"If he wants to see me, he's welcome to come."

Liam sneered. "Shall I find something to motivate you?" he asked, walking slowly toward me. "I see the female survived. You appear to have an affinity for her..." Ice ran down my spine as he neared Kat's bedroom door. "Perhaps I should finish what I started last time, before you interrupted me."

"Touch her and I'll make sure your death is slow and painful—just how she'd want it," I said. Then I whispered for my magic to come, willing it to me. I couldn't yell for help because the last thing I needed was an army of cannon fodder to come flying up the stairs. The wolves couldn't stand against him, and the enforcers remained unproven. I had no intention of finding out how they'd fare.

"Do as I tell you and I won't have to lay a hand on her, though it's tempting. I've never seen a female wolf before. So exotic. I wonder if she tastes as good as she looks."

I tried not to cringe. "What guarantee do I have that if I go, you won't come back here and attack while I'm stuck in Faerie?"

"You have the fey king's word."

"Which means fuck all to me. I want a real guarantee. Not the twisted promises of the fey."

He looked at me as though considering for the first time that I might be a worthy opponent. "You trapped me with your powers once before, did you not?" I didn't bother to answer. "Encase me in your magic again and I will be held prisoner."

"Where? Here?" I asked, my tone incredulous. "My magic will fail the moment I set foot on the other side."

"Then trap me there."

"The king will override it."

"Are you so certain he can?"

"I'm definitely not certain that he can't."

He eyed the amulet hanging around my neck, peeking out from the collar of my shirt.

"That is the fey queen's," he said, stepping closer. "Use it against me and I will be rendered unable to heed my father's call."

"Or you're trying to trick me and it'll make you more powerful."

"I'm a product of the fey king. I cannot wield her majesty's magic."

"You'll forgive me for not taking you at your word."

"What choice do you have, Piper? Either you go or they die, and the fey king will still get what he wants. He always does, you know—in due time."

He stopped short, staring at me with wide, blue, alien eyes. There was no hint of humanity in them—nothing like the wolves I'd grown to know and love. Liam might have been an original, but I doubted even a shred of that being was left untouched in the one standing before me. He was only a vessel for the fey king's anger and resentment at Knox's escape.

"Piper?" I heard Knox call from the floor below. It would be no time at all before he was in the line of fire.

"Time to decide," Liam whispered, leaning in close to me. The wickedness in his smile was plain.

I looked over my shoulder at the sound of footsteps echoing as they ascended the stairs. Time had officially run out.

"I'll go," I said, still trying to silently call my magic to me. I didn't even know what I would do with it, but I knew I would need it on the other side. If I was to face the king, I couldn't fall prey to him again.

A ripple appeared in the air beside Liam, then it

shredded a rift in the veil. He held out his hand to me and I took it. His smile spread.

"You will grow to love him, Piper. I promise…"

With those words settling on my mind, he dragged me through the portal to the sound of Knox's shouts and Grizz's bellows. Like it or not, I was going to face the fey king. And I was going alone.

22

I thought I'd be facing the fey king on my own, but I quickly realized that wasn't the case. The death grip around my wrist was evidence of that. When I landed in a vast, dark wasteland, the overcast sky split with lightning that never seemed to cease, I wasn't alone at all. Knox stood behind me, eyes wide and breathing hard. Behind him was the man-bear, staring at me over top of the alpha like I had some explaining to do for attempting to leave him behind.

Or for trying to get myself killed without him.

Instinctively I put my arms out wide, as though they alone could stop Liam from attacking if he wanted to.

"If you even try to hurt them, you're done."

Liam looked at me thoughtfully for a moment, as though my actions had surprised him.

"*Liam...*" Though the wolf with the same blue eyes as Knox stood right before the alpha, he still sounded like he couldn't believe it. I couldn't imagine what it would be like to mourn someone for lifetimes only to find out that he hadn't died; that, instead, he'd been stuck in Faerie with the psycho that created him. The horror and guilt was all over Knox's face, and Liam appeared amused by it.

Not a good sign.

"You haven't changed," Liam said, looking Knox over with keen eyes full of malice. His smile belied his true feelings, but I saw through it, as I was sure Knox did. Whoever Liam had once been was gone. In his place stood a twisted, bitter version of that being, one that wasn't at all happy to see that Knox had come for him. It seemed that ship had long ago sailed.

"I have," Knox replied, his tone still civil and full of hope. "For the better."

"How nice for you..."

"It's not too late for you," he said, stepping closer to Liam. "Life is so different on the other side."

Liam's heavy gaze fell on me, then drifted back to Knox. "I can see that."

"You could be one of us again. Foust, Brunton... we've missed you. We thought you were dead."

"Did you? And it's only taken a couple centuries for you to come and confirm that? Perhaps longer, if you count in Earth time."

"Liam, I..."

"Save it, brother. I have my purpose now. I am everything Father wanted us all to be, but you abandoned him before he could make you what I am. I will never leave him."

"He's insane, Liam. Surely you know that."

The assassin merely shrugged, the motion fluid and elegant and somehow ominous.

"I'm aware of what you did and why you did it. Father told me all about your treachery—how you sold out to the queen for *your* freedom."

"For all of us," Knox said, taking another desperate step toward Liam. Liam's evil smile widened at his approach.

"And yet you left me behind..."

"I tried to come for you," Knox argued, panic in his tone. "I tried to save you too, but..."

"But what? You had all the others so that was good enough? The cost of one was worth it to save the rest?" Liam's smile faded, leaving nothing but hostility and anger in its wake. Grizz's low growl behind me vocalized my thoughts exactly. Liam was as unstable as his master.

"Of course not," Knox said, recoiling from Liam's accusations. "It killed me to know you were still here. That the king would punish you for what I had done." He stopped for a moment, collecting himself against his rising emotions. "I swear we all thought you were dead. That's what our spies told us. That you had been tortured and killed—punished for our crimes."

"Almost, but not quite," Liam said, circling Knox methodically. His hands were clasped behind his back, but I watched as his knuckles grew whiter under his tightening grip. His anger was barely restrained. I feared for when it spilled over. "It's true that Father was angry. That he punished me severely. In fact, I do believe he'd have killed me—I could see it in his eyes as he lifted my limp head from the ground after a beating—but something changed. He decided to let me live. From that point on, I was reborn in his image, gifted with magic the rest of you never were or will be." Not good. So not good. "It's ironic that you sold your soul for your freedom, and all you did was trade one master for another." Again, his weighted gaze fell on me.

"I'm not his master," I said, stepping up to Knox's side. "We're equals. A team."

For a moment Liam's anger faltered, letting disbelief flash across his face. Knox didn't miss it.

"Do not confuse alliance with servitude, brother," Knox said, his tone full of warning. "Come back with us. Be one of us again. Piper can help you—help heal you."

Liam hesitated for a moment, then let loose a laugh full of acid and pain.

"I don't need your whore's help. I'm as whole as I need to be. And I'm not leaving." He leaned in closer to Knox, and I felt Grizz move behind me, stepping between the alpha and me. He had Knox's back, come what may. "And neither are you."

Knox stiffened and Grizz pressed closer, the two of them a united front against the twisted wolf turned magical weapon for the fey king. But I wouldn't be left out of the fight. If Liam so much as raised a finger against Knox, he'd learn exactly what this whore could do.

Death would be a mercy.

I glanced over my shoulder to where the portal we'd come through stood. Then I pinned a vengeful stare on Liam. It seemed to only amuse him further.

"They're leaving. Try to stop them and it'll mean your end."

Liam cocked his head, an alien expression on his face. He seemed truly baffled by my actions. Like he couldn't begin to comprehend them.

"You would die for them?"

"I would die for anyone I love." His eyes narrowed. "And if you were still one of Knox's pack, I would die for you too."

A genuine, albeit mildly psychotic, smile spread across his face.

"I must say, brother, she is both exotic and entertaining. I think I'll keep her once the king is done with her—he always tires of his playthings. You can consider it compensation for the wrongs you've done me."

Liam's hand shot out toward me, the speed of it mind-blowing. Before I knew it, he had his arm around my waist, dragging me away from the guys. Knox's eyes glowed yellow and his claws extended from his fingers. He lunged for us, but was stopped with a single command.

"Stand down." The fey king's voice rang out through the air with such power it was awe-inspiring. Though I wasn't one of his creations, I still felt it. Knox froze in place, the strain visible in his expression as he tried to fight against the king's directive and failed.

Grizz, not hindered by the same connection that bound Knox to the king, charged Liam as I struggled to call my magic. Something about being in Liam's hold seemed to choke it off. What little I had was lost as he squeezed me tighter. If it came down to a battle of strength, I was totally fucked.

Liam laughed at Grizz until the man-bear clotheslined him across the throat, just above my head. He staggered back a step or two, dragging me along with him. Grizz grabbed hold of me and ripped me from Liam's grasp. He threw me aside so he could face the demented wolf, who now stood facing off against him. Fear shot up my spine, knowing that Grizz couldn't stand against Liam for long, if at all. And with Knox incapacitated and my magic weak at best, things started to look bleaker by the second.

I ran to Knox's side, wrapping my hand around his wrist and pressing the amulet to his chest. Liam had said the fey queen's magic would interfere with the king's, and I prayed that he wasn't full of shit. Much to my surprise, Knox started to move. I could feel that a part of him was still tethered to the king's command, but the rest of him fought it like a man possessed. Moments later Knox was free, running to aid Grizz. Together they formed a wall to keep Liam at bay while I turned my attention to the fey king. Maybe I didn't have the power to fight him—maybe it was still broken—but negotiating had long been a skill of mine, honed to perfection during my years surviving alone on the streets. I could wield that against him either way.

And I still had the amulet in case all else failed.

"I did not expect you to bring your entourage with you," the fey king said, coming out of a pocket of shadow. "All the better for me."

"You summoned me," I said, every ounce of disdain I felt for him dripping from my words.

"And you came like a good girl. Is it door number three, then?" he asked, stepping closer. I could feel the rush of sexuality flowing from him and I struggled to fight it. "I can give you the freedom to be who you really are."

"So can they," I replied through gritted teeth.

"Can they now?" he asked, feigning interest. "From all I have heard and the bits I have seen, you look like you're collateral damage in their war. Join me and all the pressure goes away."

"I am happy where I am." My fists balled at my sides.

"You'd be happier *here*."

"You can't give me something I already have," I said, staring down his beautiful face.

He smiled at my insolence.

"Maybe. Maybe not. But I can certainly take it away..."

"This is between you and me," Knox interrupted, reaching back to take my hand in his. I felt a tiny rush of power, but nothing like I had in the past when we'd joined forces. Something was wrong. As though my fears were written all over my face, the fey king smiled.

"You look surprised by something, Piper. Is my realm not everything you imagined it would be? Are you disappointed by your new home?"

"I told you, I won't be staying," I said, looking back over my shoulder again at the portal. I heard his laugh envelop me as the small tear in the veil sewed itself shut.

"I'm afraid you will be. *All* of you." He gave Knox a pointed look before returning his focus to me. "Now, it's time you and I sort out how we can take down the queen."

"You can't, Piper," Knox said quietly in my ear.

"Of course she can't," the fey king said, his expression incredulous. "Not without my help."

"Remember what we talked about with Drake the other day?" Knox said, ignoring the king. "About Reinhardt and what his death meant?"

I looked up at him, reading between the lines. I didn't like what I found. If the fey queen died, she would need a successor. And since the whereabouts of my mother, or anyone else from her line, were unknown, that would leave me to fill the vacancy, tethering me to Faerie—and making me the fey king's next target. All part of his plan, no doubt.

"What will it be, Piper?" the king asked. This time, I could feel the press of magic in his words, making me want to obey him. Knox's hand squeezed mine tighter, and my head cleared.

"No," I said softly, trying to silently call upon the magic in the amulet to help us out. I only needed enough to create a portal and run. Wherever it led, it would be safer than where we were. Even if it landed us in the queen's lap. "I won't do it."

His calm, beautiful façade fell just enough to show the wretched evil it belied. The true fey king.

"You *will*," he replied, his tone calm but full of malice. It seemed the fey king—like the queen—did not enjoy being rebuffed. "Or I will make you." He turned his attention to Grizz and Knox, and my heart fell to my stomach. "Liam," he called as if beckoning a child to him. "If you'd be so kind." The assassin's eyes fell upon his "brother" and I could see them dilate with anticipation. In a flash, he lunged for Knox. I threw my hand out to ward him off, and to my surprise, a fireball flew out from my palm, striking the rogue wolf in the chest. It knocked him backward, charring his exposed skin. He looked down at it as though I'd only served to annoy him, then set his sights once again on Knox.

"Interesting," the king purred, looking at me like I was more than he'd expected. Like he had underestimated me. "*Knox*." The weight of his name shot a ripple through the air around us. Like a puppet on a string, Knox drew his chest up as his body went rigid. This was the moment he'd feared. The one when the king would use his connection against us. He should have never returned to the king's realm. "If you won't help me willingly, Piper, then you will do it by force. But understand one thing—you *will* do my bidding. All my pets do."

With a flick of his wrist, Knox released my hand and growled at me as though I were the enemy in his presence. Grizz grabbed his shoulder, his massive hand encasing it whole, but Knox simply turned and threw the man-bear across the field. I was certain the fall would kill him. Knox's powers had never been that strong on Earth. I swallowed hard at the realization.

He was as formidable as Liam in his true world.

"Knox," I said, my tone low and calm. I pulled the

amulet over my head and clutched it in my hands, rubbing it like a rosary. "Knox... it's me. You have to fight this. He may have created you, but you said it yourself—we were fated. And no power of his can override fate."

I heard the king's laughter behind me, and I did my best to ignore it.

I saw Knox's hand raise in a fist, but there was a shake to it. A resistance. I looked into his ice blue eyes and searched for any sign of recognition. Somewhere deep inside, I found it.

"If you will not help me, I have no use for you, Piper," the king warned. Knox stepped closer, claws extending from his fingers. "You know it will destroy him if he kills you, don't you? He'll be trapped here with his guilt for an eternity..."

"Fight this," I whispered to him, pressing the amulet against his chest. He faltered for a moment before stepping back and knocking it from my hand.

"Hit her," the fey king ordered, his voice cruel and commanding. The bite of stinging flesh shot through me. I heard Grizz growl in the distance and felt oddly relieved in that moment. At least he was okay—for now. "Again!" the king shouted. Open palm met cheek, this time with the slicing of delicate flesh under the sharp tips of his claws.

Tears ran down my face as Knox methodically—and slowly—attacked me. I tried to defend myself, but he just kept moving, changing his angle of attack. I tried to call my magic, but nothing came. Nothing at all. I dropped to the ground to search for the amulet, still weathering Knox's blows.

The king looked on as though bored by the whole thing. Liam, however, was intrigued. Whether it was morbid curiosity or true fascination with my behavior, he took a step closer to us, watching his brother slowly beat me to death. I wondered if he would join in.

With another crushing blow, I lurched forward onto my stomach, my arms and legs sprawled out. My hand grabbed Knox's ankle and I squeezed it hard. There was a definite pause in his otherwise rhythmic beating. I focused on the connection we had—the one I'd always felt around Knox— and I channeled the shit out of it into him. I looked up at him through matted hair to see wide eyes staring back at me as he stood frozen, a look of horror on his face as he took in what he'd done.

The fey king laughed.

"How touching. You think love can save you," he said, bitterness dripping from his words. "Love is an illusion. A lie. The only true power you can hold over another, besides power itself, is fear and brutality." The fey king stepped closer, and I tried to reach the amulet, fingers scraping the barren earth as they clawed for it. If we were to have any chance at all to get out of there, I needed it. "Knox was able to escape my dominance once. I was careless back then, and I suffered because of it. But I've taken a *lesser* creature and made him everything I'd hoped Knox would one day become. The perfect killing machine." My eyes fell to Liam, who stood next to his creator, staring down at my hand where it gripped Knox. "But now my prodigal son has returned and I can continue my work. He will be even better than Liam. The firstborn is always the best, you know. And I will prove it." He put his hand on Knox's shoulder and squeezed it hard. "Kill her."

Something in Knox's eyes twitched just as my fingertips grazed the amulet.

"I love you," I whispered to him, scrambling to my feet while focusing on the magic in the amulet. Knox's head slowly swiveled toward the king, then back to me. Slowly raising a clawed hand, he drew his jerky finger gently along my cheek.

Then, looking at his father, he put it to his own throat and sliced it wide open.

23

Blood drained from my face at the rate it poured from Knox's body. Watching the pool of red below him grow was surreal. Until it wasn't. The second my mind reconciled what I was seeing with what it meant, I screamed his name.

"Knox!"

No response.

I heard the fey king laughing somewhere behind me, and my blood boiled. If I'd had my full powers, I'd have ripped his head from his body with a flick of my wrist. But I didn't have them, which would soon prove to be a problem for other reasons.

Grizz looked at me as he scooped the alpha's limp, dripping form from the ground. I clutched the amulet in my hand and squeezed it, trying to milk every bit of magic I could from it—hoping it would give me enough power to incapacitate the king long enough to make a break for it. Hopefully it would help guide us to its creator's land.

"He always was a clever one," the fey king said, the amusement in his tone making me see red. "Shame he found a way around my directive. Losing him is *disappointing*."

"He isn't yours to lose," I said, my voice low and threatening. "He never was."

The king cocked his head. "You think the wolves are *yours*."

"I think I've earned their loyalty, unlike you, who forces them into submission."

Grizz made a noise behind me, a desperate plea to get out of there before we ran out of time—if we had any to start with.

"Can I force you into submission, I wonder?" the fey king said, stepping closer to me.

My hand clutched the amulet that warmed in my grasp, begging me to draw every last ounce of power it had. I had one shot to take the king down. One shot to take him by surprise if I wanted Knox to have any chance of surviving. With a deep breath, I thought about what Drake had taught me. I thought about all I'd lost—and all I still stood to lose. There was no way I would let the fey king accomplish what the fey queen had attempted. He couldn't take someone I loved from me.

Over my dead fucking body.

"Did you mean what you said?" Liam asked, his empty eyes drifting from Knox's dying body to me. "About the wolves?"

I nodded once, tears welling in my eyes.

"There is nothing I wouldn't do for them," I replied, anger and sadness thick in my tone.

It was then that I saw something in Liam's eyes that reminded me of Knox. For that brief moment in time, he looked like his brother. Softer. Kinder. A hint of what he'd once been before the king destroyed him.

Then he smiled. "Time to take him home," he said before launching himself at the fey king. For a moment, I was paralyzed by the sight. Then Grizz grabbed my arm and started running in the opposite direction. The amulet grew brighter with every step.

I heard an inhuman cry from behind us, and I turned to see the fey king stand. Without thinking, I stopped and threw my hands up, shooting a ball of fire toward him. It grew as it sped across the distance and then exploded, raining down upon him and Liam.

We continued running, not daring to look back again. At best, I'd incapacitated the king. At worst, I'd just pissed him off. Either way, it didn't matter. We had to get to away.

As we ran, I could feel the familiar tug of magic that I'd felt before in Faerie grow stronger. We were closing in on the border with every step. Relief flooded me, knowing that it wouldn't be long before my powers would return and I could save Knox. I feared he wouldn't make it home without being healed first.

"Grizz! Is he still alive?" I shouted as we hit a clearing. The bear grunted something at me in return that I took as a yes. I wanted to let out a sigh of relief, but something I saw in the distance cut off my breath altogether. Standing in a long line across what I had to assume was the border between the king's dark land and the lush territory of the queen was her royal army, with her majesty, the queen herself, standing in the middle.

We instinctively slowed, Grizz and I both knowing what her presence meant. But then a calm and eerie voice from behind us spurred us on. The king was coming. We were between a rock and a hard place.

Where my fey powers lay, an army awaited.

Where my fey powers were null, certain death approached.

"Such a conundrum," the fey queen said, the joy she took in my predicament duly noted. "If you do not give him what he wants, he will kill you, my dear. Make no mistake about that. And your wolf—poor Trevor—he is not long for this world, or yours, for that matter. Tick tock, Piper. Time to make a decision."

Grizz looked down at me, his wide eyes awaiting my call.

I turned to find the fey king closing in on us, the feral rage in his eyes plain even from a distance. Once he unleashed his fury, there would be no stopping him. I was no match for him on his turf. And Grizz was no match for him anywhere.

Knowing that, the grizzly-turned-man put himself between me and the most imminent threat, looking over his shoulder at me as if to say goodbye.

"Not a fucking chance," I growled at him. I swear to God he smiled back. "I want amnesty," I shouted at the queen, who looked amused by my boldness.

"You shall not have it. But I will do this. If you come now, you and your companions will not be harmed." I took a step closer to her and her army. "But you will owe me a favor— one I can collect at any time."

My hackles rose.

I knew exactly what that favor would mean—me as her prisoner in Faerie. I opened my mouth to argue, but then I saw Knox's limp arm and how grey it had turned, and I knew that I would agree to her terms, even though I knew that he and Merc would never forgive me for it. It was a non-choice, really. A necessary evil.

I grabbed Grizz's arm and dragged him toward the invisible divide and the army awaiting us there. I saw the king throw his arm up to hurl magic at us, but it crashed into a force field of sorts and dissipated without impact. Whether it was the queen's doing or the natural divide of power between the two lands, I didn't care; all I cared about was Knox. Grizz gently laid the alpha down on the ground, and I crashed to my knees at his side.

As I put my hands on Knox, Grizz snatched the amulet from me and placed it around his neck for safekeeping—or to mock the fey queen with her gift to the warlocks. He stood between the queen and me while I tried to bring Knox back. He wasn't dead, but he was perilously close.

"Heal him," I said, low and strong. Instead of a flash of light, I felt the ground shake beneath us. Roots snaked out of the ground and wrapped themselves around his body. I could feel them pulsate with magic. Magic far older and stronger than any I'd ever called on Earth or in Faerie. It visibly coursed through them into Knox. With every throb, I could see his skin brighten and his color return. It was as though Faerie was beating his heart for him.

"You cannot fully heal him here," the fey queen said from behind me in her typical superior tone. "He is a child of the king—his creation. It was his magic that called him into being. It is his magic he needs to fully repair. My realm is keeping him alive. Nothing more."

Grizz growled at her, taking offense at her trickery.

I asked that same magic to heal me. It did, my injuries disappearing in an instant, and I shot to my feet, anger thrumming through my veins like the magic through Knox's. I could hardly hear her words over the pounding in my ears. Favor be damned. The queen and I were going to end things right then and there.

But the fey king had other plans.

"That is what you get for trusting my wife," he said, toeing the line between their realms.

"I trust neither of you," I replied, staring at his wife, the more imminent threat before me.

"The wolf is mine. Only I can heal him. Give him to me."

I opened my mouth to reply, but Grizz's roar was answer enough. Knox wasn't going anywhere on his watch.

"Says the one who just tried to kill him," the queen said, as though the comment had been directed at her. "I swear, Phineas, you don't know how to treat your toys."

"Just as you don't know how to treat your beloved," he volleyed right back at her.

"Will you shut up!" I shouted over my shoulder at him. "You're distracting me."

"From what, dear Piper? Staring down the queen of the fey? Has her beauty got you entranced?"

"Hardly. But the thought of her death is appealing."

His silence made me nervous, and I turned to look at him. All I saw was wild amusement in his eyes; the kind that only a person privy to a secret could hold. Kingston had looked at me that way before. So had the queen of the fey.

"You want to kill her yourself, do you?" His request for clarification was for show, given the gleam in his eyes. He clearly knew the answer and it amused him. "Well, well..." he mused. "What a predicament you are in, then, Piper." Though it was apparent that the king knew what he was talking about, I couldn't help but wonder whether the queen did. I looked over my shoulder at her. There was a wariness in her eyes, as if she too was trying to puzzle out his implication. "I'll tell you what," he started, moving as close as he dared to the boundary. "I'll forgive this recent transgression if you agree to join me. I can do something you cannot do yourself. Something you want badly. I can see her death in your eyes. I can give that to you."

"I can give it to myself, asshole."

"Sadly, my dear, you cannot. You see, fey royalty had a rather ugly past—one full of murder and regicide. It came to the point where no fey royal was safe from another. Our lines most certainly would have been wiped out if we hadn't been forced to stop killing our children. Or our parents." Realization started to dawn on me, and I looked over at the queen, whose expression had changed from skepticism to disbelief.

"She cannot be..."

"Oh, she can, my love."

"What?" I asked, my head whipping back and forth on my neck as I tried to glean something from either one of them. "You're saying I can't kill her because I'm descended from her? Then why does she keep trying to kill me and those I love?"

The fey king smiled a smile that would have terrified Satan himself. "She's not trying to kill you, Piper. She already did that once." His eyes darted down to Knox and lingered for a moment before shifting back to me. "Seems her attempt failed."

"Of course it did," I said, my mind turning over at a rapid rate. "I wouldn't exist if she'd killed that child. I'd have never been born."

His beautifully frightening smile widened. "Who do you think you are, Piper?"

"I'm the daughter of Reinhardt, warlock lord."

"And your mother?"

"My mother was born of the child this bitch tried to have killed."

The fey king's laughter rang out around us, hemming us

in with its harsh, biting tone. When he finally stopped, he pinned deadly serious eyes on me, and then the queen. Though I knew he was addressing me, those eyes were all for her.

"I harbored that child in my realm, Piper. Did Knox tell you that? Did you know that I allowed her to exist on my side until I saw fit to make her leave?" He paused for a moment to assess my reaction. "I sent her away when I felt the queen's spies were getting too close. When I thought the child would be safer on Earth. Knowing her lineage, I had no reason to fear for her safety there. She could grow among the mortals until she realized that she was so much more than them." I could feel my chest tightening as he spoke—a visceral reaction to the subtext of his words. This scenario hit too close to home.

"The child," I started, losing my voice for a second. "Where was the child taken?"

He reveled in my expression. "I did not bother to inquire until long after she had left, but my understanding is that she was taken to one of those unwanted children's hovels—an orphanage?" My heart stopped beating. "It was quite some time ago, though. Unimportant details like this tend to leave me. And it's always so confusing, you know, reconciling Earth time with that in Faerie... the inconsistencies can be daunting for even the most cunning mind."

"How long ago?" I asked, my words merely a whisper.

"If I had to guess, I would say twenty Earth years—give or take a few. Like I said, it's just so hard to keep track of the conversion. Time moves *very slowly* on this side of Faerie," he said with a malicious smile. "Decades could pass on Earth while only one year would here in my realm."

I stared at him wide-eyed and breathless, my mind fracturing into pieces. Decades of human years could pass in a single year there. A toddler could have aged only a couple of years in, say, sixty or so Earth years.

The truth barreled into me.

"I'm the child," I said, my voice gathering strength as I spoke. "The child you ordered to be killed." I wheeled around on my mother, ready to bring my wrath down upon her—but I couldn't. Just as she could not directly bring hers down upon me. For a moment, I wondered whether there were ways to circumvent that rule. Then I wondered if the fey king would be willing to tell me.

"I wasn't certain," she said by way of reply. "When I learned of a Magical with strange abilities—a strong connection to nature—I wondered if Trevor had not done his job after all. The more I learned of this rare creature, the more I suspected there was a connection. I needed to see for myself."

"So you kidnapped Merc to draw me out."

"Technically he came willingly, remember?"

"To spare me!" I shouted at her, launching to my feet.

"An action that only heightened my suspicions."

"Well now you know the truth, you fucking bitch."

Her expression hardened. "And so do you."

"This is touching, really," the fey king said, sounding anything but moved. "But the question now is, what will you two do, Piper? How my mind does wonder..."

"I know what I'm doing," I said, turning to Grizz. I jerked my head toward the ground, indicating he should scoop up Knox so we could bugger off. But when the man-bear went to lift him, Faerie wouldn't comply. The roots gripped Knox tighter, nearly pulling him down into the ground. I watched as he inched lower and lower, the ground slowly swallowing him until very little of him remained visible. I knew in my heart that if he disappeared, he would never return.

"STOP!" I shouted, and his movement ceased. "Release him. Now!" My demand made the ground below me quake. The fey king's eyes delighted in my power, as though he had already figured out how to bring it to his side. The queen, however, looked far less impressed.

"We will be keeping him, I think," she said, and once again he started to sink into the mossy earth.

"I will be taking him as we agreed," I growled. A cool metal weight was pressed into my hand, and I turned to find Grizz handing me the amulet. I smiled up at him. The bear was clutch. I closed my eyes and took a deep breath, channeling all my childhood rage and current anger. Then I unleashed it on the queen and her army.

"Be gone!" I screamed, and seconds later a wall of wind slammed into them, driving them across the opening and through the trees. I turned my attention to Knox and put my hand on his chest. "Release him to me." Like obedient animals, the branches uncoiled from around him and disappeared back into the ground. In a second, Grizz had Knox in his arms, looking to me for our next move.

I reached into that dark place inside of me—the one I'd found when I shredded a hole in the veil between worlds—and found the magic necessary to repeat the act. With an open hand, I swiped at the air in front of me. It fell open like a torn curtain, the opening a crooked mouth of sorts. I practically shoved Grizz's massive form through it before I moved to follow him.

"I regret attempting to kill you," the fey king said, drawing my attention. There was insanity in his gaze, and a shot of cold went down my spine at the sight of him. "Until we meet again... and we will, you know. That kiss we shared—when I called for you and you came—has bound us, Piper... I can get to you anywhere." He turned to walk away like nothing had ever happened between us. Like he hadn't tried to murder me and ruined me with the truth of who my mother was.

Grizz growled at me through the makeshift portal, and I managed to climb through it. We emerged at the edge of the woods on the enforcers' property. Even if the mansion in the distance hadn't given our location away, the wall of approaching wolves would have. They poured around the corner of the mansion, running toward us. The look on their faces was a mix of relief and fear. They could feel Knox's return.

Apparently they could also feel just how uncertain his condition was.

I put my hands on Knox while Grizz held him and called forth my healing ability. This time, it came without hesitation, the familiar bright light exploding all around us. Moments later, I felt Knox stir beneath my hands. I spared a glance over my shoulder to where the wolves had stopped, huddling together only feet away. Foust had called them to a halt to give me space. Or maybe he hadn't been ready to face what he might find if he got too close.

"Piper," Knox called, his voice weak and raspy. Not entirely surprising, given what he'd done.

"We're home," I said softly, pushing his wild blond hair out of his face. "And it seems like your boys are excited to see you."

Grizz placed Knox down on his feet, and the alpha's arms were immediately around me, crushing me against him.

"I'm so sorry, Piper."

"It's not your fault, Knox. We knew it could happen," I said, hugging him tighter. "And you fought it and won. But don't ever do that to me again, do you hear me? You can't leave me..."

A tiny growl from Grizz drew our attention. Knox loosened his hold just enough to look over his shoulder at the bear, but Grizz didn't seem satisfied with that. He grabbed the werewolf and bear-hugged him (no pun intended), picking him up off the ground.

"I'm good, man," Knox said, a wheeze in his voice due to his constricted breathing. "I won't leave you either."

"Okay, big guy. Time to put him down."

The bear shot me a look that told me I didn't get to make that call, but I put my hands on my hips and cocked my head at him, and he knew he was going to lose. With a huff, he did as I'd asked.

"What happened?" Foust asked, coming up behind me. He was flanked by Jagger and Brunton, the others hanging back a bit, waiting for the nod to come forward and inspect their leader.

Knox and I looked at each other the way Jase and Dean often did and had a silent conversation of our own; the kind where we both sifted through the information to determine what didn't need to be shared just yet, coming to our own conclusions about how much editing was necessary.

"That's what I want to know!" Kat shouted, barreling through the boys to wrap her arms around me. "I swear on all that's holy, Piper, if you ever disappear like that again, I'll kill you myself." Grizz let out a warning growl. "Oh c'mon, big guy. You know I'm bullshitting." His expression didn't change. Kat let out a sigh and released me before making her way over to him and giving him a hug. His irritated expression disappeared in an instant. I smiled to myself at the sight of the two of them and their odd-couple friendship.

The rest of the pack came over to join us, and I soon found myself swarmed by male bodies trying to get to Knox, doing their weird half-hug man thing and clapping one another on the back. While they greeted their alpha, I slowly backed my way out of the group. Knox and I still had things to talk about, but his boys needed him and I didn't want to get in the way. They had their own things to talk about.

I'd almost made it through the last of them when a hand caught my arm, holding me in place. I turned to find Brunton looking at me, his eyes surveying me.

"How bad was it?" he asked.

I hesitated. "Bad, but it's going to be okay."

I tried to pull my arm from his grip, but he held strong, his expression softening slightly.

"Thanks, Piper... for bringing him back."

I cracked a smile. "No problem. Besides, I think I'm getting the hang of Faerie rescue missions now."

He let out a harsh laugh. "Maybe you should lay off for a bit."

I shrugged. "I can't help that trouble keeps finding me."

Wasn't that the damn truth—and there was no end in sight.

"Nah, he said with a shake of his head. "I guess you can't."

He gave me a quick nod then let me go, disappearing into the pack.

I took that opportunity to resume my escape, headed for the mansion. I crossed the empty lawn, enjoying the smell of the air and the familiar sounds of the property and the feeling that, for the moment, everything was okay. Yes, I was the daughter of the fey queen—a detail I was going to have to reveal to everyone soon enough—but for that night, I would let that truth hide in the shadows. Because beyond that darkness, there was an uncertain future, riddled with backlash from past events. I knew that, regardless of whether or not I could kill the fey queen myself, she had to die. Possibly the fey king too. And their deaths would create vacancies in the positions of power in Faerie—roles that would need to be filled by someone.

And that someone was me.

I'D BARELY SET foot in the foyer when Jase and Dean swarmed me, engulfing me in the world's most awkward hug sandwich. Smashed between those two was the epitome of most girls' dreams, but to me it was just claustrophobic.

"Could you two learn to take turns?" I shouted, my voice muffled by someone's chest. They released me just enough so I wasn't crushed.

"Piper," Jase started, sounding scared. "We need you—"

"Like now," Dean finished for his brother.

"What's wrong?" I asked, the tension surrounding them slowly creeping up my spine. "Where is Merc?"

"Come with us."

Jase took my arm gently in his and ghosted me to the basement. Dean appeared seconds later. And that's when I heard the muffled cries somewhere past the double doors at the end of the basement hallway.

"Where are we going?" I asked, knowing that there were only a few options.

"You have to stop him," Jase said, his voice low and cold. "We can't reach him."

"Stop him from what?" I asked, starting toward those doors. I couldn't hide the fear in my voice. "Is he the reason you have those bruises on your face?" Silence. "Tell me right now, you two, what the fuck is going on?"

"He's gone off the deep end," Dean finally said.

"With the king..." Jase added.

I sprinted down the hall toward the infirmary. Jase led the way to a locked door on the far end of the tiled room. It led to an underground passage that eventually ended in a single locked cell. It was then that I pieced together exactly where we were headed. The king was still Merc's prisoner— providing he was still alive.

"Why would you leave him alone with him?" I shouted at them, panic straining my voice.

"We didn't know he was here until you disappeared and Merc snapped. We followed him downstairs and discovered where the king has been imprisoned this whole time."

"MERC!" I screamed, hoping that he could hear me; that he wasn't lost to his madness already. His real, true madness this time.

By the time we reached the king's prison, I could hear Merc's shouts and the king's cries. Whatever Merc was doing to him, it sounded horrific. The dark spot deep inside of me smiled at the noise.

"Merc!" I screamed again, hoping to stop him before he did something stupid—something irreparable and soul-crushing to us both. His words rang through my mind as we ran toward him. "*The king cannot be bound to anyone*" played on a tormenting loop with every step I took until I rounded the king's cell and found Merc there, covered in blood, his eyes wide and feral, and without any shred of the man I loved in them.

"What have you done?" I whispered, staring at the gory sight before me. Jase and Dean rushed past me to the king, checking their father for any signs of life. But from the way his head lolled off to the side at an impossible angle, I knew they'd find none. Even though the vampires had no heart-beats—no pulses to check—a severed head was sign enough that he wouldn't be springing to his feet any time soon. The vampire king was really and truly dead.

And so was my bond to Merc.

24

It was terrifying to stand before Merc and stare into those cold, dead eyes. Eyes that could not tell friend from foe. Eyes that didn't really seem to see anything at all but the color of blood. But I wasn't the same girl standing before him in that dungeon.

I was the princess of Faerie.

Clinging to that knowledge, I took a step closer to him.

"Piper," Jase shouted, jumping between Merc and me. But his attempt to intercede was pointless. With a brutal show of force, Merc knocked his brother across the room. Jase ghosted just before his massive frame could crash into the cinderblock wall. Dean moved then, preparing to pick up where Jase had left off, but I stopped him with a single look.

"He will not hurt me," I said, but that time I meant it. Because if he tried to, he'd incur my wrath. Merc's wild eyes seemed to focus on me as I took a step forward—as if he was coming back to himself a bit. I kept my pace slow and my body neutral, but inside I was preparing to do what I had to in order to avoid a repeat of the last time we'd fought. "I'm okay," I said softly, taking another step. "I know why you're so angry. I know you think something awful happened to me and you blame yourself for that—blame our bond for the loss of my magic—but I'm fine, Merc. I'm *home*."

A flicker of recognition gleamed in his eyes. I dared to move closer.

"He had to die," he said, his voice distant and detached. "I had to end it."

"Why?" I asked, nearing him. I could have touched his chest if I'd reached out, but my hands remained at my sides. Merc was no longer my mate. Our bond had been severed. And though I felt no differently toward him, I couldn't guarantee he felt the same. Our bond had practically owned him before. I wondered how he would feel in its absence. "Why did he have to die?"

"Because," he said, as though that word were answer enough. "He was the cause of it all. Of everything." Those dark and distant eyes focused in on me with laser accuracy.

"He knew I was the queen's daughter..."

A hint of sorrow bled into his harsh expression.

"*Yes*." He stared at me, silent for a long moment before continuing. "I had always suspected as much, but when the fey queen came for me, I knew it was true. By then I had been able to retrace your childhood and the fey that had sheltered you. I knew where you had been before arriving on Earth. I knew it all."

"Why didn't you tell me?" My words were barely audible, hurt and anger choking them off.

"What did you have to gain from that knowledge, Piper? What good would have come of it? Your ignorance was what kept you safe."

"I don't need to be protected..."

"You cannot blame me for wanting to."

By the time he finished his sentence, I could tell that the real Merc had returned, and he was devastated by what he had done.

"And this?" I asked, pointing to the king's corpse. "Was this to protect me too? To protect me from *you*? From your effect on me?"

He nodded. "And now I will pay the consequences for it." He cast a heavy glance down at his dead predecessor. The shoes he would have to fill.

"Merc, I..."

"I'm glad you are home safe, Piper." He hesitated for a moment. "And the others?"

"Grizz is fine. Knox is... he'll be okay soon."

"We all will," he said, leveling me with a sad look before walking past me to exit the prison cell the king had occupied.

"Where are you going?" I asked as he passed through the door.

"To my new home," he replied, unable or unwilling to look back at me.

His words were a punch to my stomach.

"Merc, we'll find a way around this," Dean said, coming to stand beside me. I could hear the pain in his voice. He knew what his brother's madness had cost him.

"I'm afraid that is impossible, brother."

"Merc!" I called out to him as he disappeared around the corner. I ran after him, feeling like my delayed emotions had slammed into me all at once. The finality of the situation was causing me to panic. "You can't leave!" He paused. "I need you..."

"You need what I can do for you, Piper. Nothing more."

Those words tore right through me, leaving a gaping hole in their wake.

"How can you possibly think that?"

"I will be there whenever you need me. *Always*."

Without another word he disappeared into the ether, leaving me alone in the hallway with a growing sense of disbelief and a broken heart. With one act of vengeance— one slip of control when it was needed most—everything between us had shattered into a million pieces. And I could see no way to fix it. The vampire king could not be bonded to anyone, that much was certain. What I didn't know was whether that was by necessity or curse.

But I had a sneaking suspicion I knew someone who did.

If anyone had the answer I sought, it would be the fey queen. Magical rules and loopholes were her specialty. If there were a solution to be found, she'd know what it was. The only minor problem with that plan was the unlikelihood that she would share that information with me, and if she did, at what cost. I already owed her a favor. And since the only other person I knew that had ever been in that position had been ordered to kill a baby, it didn't bode well. Putting myself in a position to owe her another was lunacy. Crazy or not, though, something had to fix the mess Merc's outrage had caused. Something had to free him of the noose around his neck. I feared that, in his role as vampire king, he would slip farther and farther away from me, and from sanity. He'd said once that he felt alive around me—that the light within me pulled him from a dark place. Without that presence in his life, I feared for what would become of him, and if I was being brutally honest, me in the end. He was part of the balancing equation that kept my powers in check. Losing that wasn't an option, given all that had transpired over the past two weeks.

But how to keep it seemed an impossible question to answer.

25

We burned the body in the back yard, but there was no ceremony this time, no pomp and circumstance. The former vampire king got exactly what he deserved—fire, then nothing. Most of the enforcers didn't attend, and Merc was nowhere to be found. When it was over, I went over to the ashes and spit in them.

The wolves had kept their distance, but they were all outside waiting for it to be over. As I walked away from the pyre, Knox approached, his expression tight and resolved.

"Piper," he said, and my heart dropped. He'd used his business voice on me, which never boded well.

"What now?' I asked, wanting to cut to the chase. He frowned for a moment, his brows furrowed with frustration. Then he took a deep breath.

"You need to get Merc."

So not what I'd expected him to say. "Excuse me?"

"You heard what I said."

"Oh, I *heard* you. I just don't *understand* you."

"You need him. I get it. I really do. And even though I hate it, Drake is right. You can't survive without both of us in your life. I get that he's punishing himself for going off the deep end and killing the king, but he needs to suck it the fuck up. So he's the vampire king—so what? He can do that and still have your back."

If only it were that simple.

"Knox... I need to tell you something."

"Aww shit..."

"Merc severed our bond when he killed the king."

Silence.

"Are you fucking kidding me?" I shook my head. "Why would he do that? That doesn't even make sense."

"He didn't mean to—at least I don't think he did. He didn't explain himself, but I think he thought the worst and snapped. He knew I was the queen's daughter—and he knew his father knew too. He blamed him for everything that happened to me. And when he thought I wouldn't be returning from the fey king's realm..."

Knox let out a low whistle. "He fucking lost it," Knox said, raking his hand through his hair. "He's been known to do that. But I can't say I blame him this time. I would've."

"I know. You two are similar in that regard."

"When it comes to you, yeah. We always will be." He looked at me thoughtfully, awaiting a response. When he realized I didn't have one for him, he moved on. "So, do you think he can still keep you from burning out?"

I swallowed hard.

"I don't know."

"Well we're about to find out," another male called out from across the lawn. I looked past Knox to find Drake approaching. The irritation in his expression was plain even from far away. "Let's go. I think it's time we paid the new vampire king our respects."

ﾞ♣ﾞ

I STOOD outside the king's mansion, doing all I could to calm my nerves. Part of my anxiety was due to the PTSD I had from the parties I'd attended there. The rest was from my growing unease regarding Merc and me—and his current state of mind.

"Just kick it in," Kat said to Knox, who stood at my side. Apparently he didn't need much prodding, because he took one step back and shot his leg out, breaking the door clean off its hinges with a single blow. Why there hadn't been more to stop it—magically speaking—was curious at best. At worst, it was a sign that Merc didn't give a shit.

And that just wouldn't do.

"Merc!" I shouted as I stepped through the front door, the others following behind me. Knox was practically on top of me he was walking so close, and Drake wasn't far behind him. I could hear Kat laughing about something behind them—most likely about their position—and Grizz snorting in agreement. Those two would be the death of me one day, I just knew it.

I made my way through the parts of the house I knew until I came to the office where I'd attacked the previous king. There, sitting at the same desk, sat Merc, his fingers tented in front of his mouth. He looked deep in thought.

"Hey," I said cautiously, entering the room uninvited. "We came to see you."

He looked up at me, dark eyes empty and cold, and said nothing.

I turned to Drake, who had come to stand at my right, and silently beseeched him. He'd quickly grown to be the voice of reason in so many situations. I prayed he'd know what to say and do.

"Piper," Drake said, his eyes turning to Merc. "Provoke him."

"I'm sorry, *what*?"

"I said provoke him. Get mad at him. *Attack* him." This was so not the plan I'd bargained for. I made a mental note to revoke Drake's "voice of reason" title.

Merc slowly rose from his chair, his eyes boring holes into my soul, and walked around his desk to stand before me. I could feel Knox tense at my left and Grizz's hand on my back from behind me, but I knew they would wait for me to make the first move.

"You said you'd be there when I needed you," I said, taking a step closer to him, much to Grizz's dismay. "Well I need you." I looked over my shoulder at our tiny crew, then back at him. "We all do. We can't deal with the fey royals without you."

He cocked his head at me, assessing me silently. I wondered if he'd resumed his selectively mute status. If yes, getting pissed at him would prove easier than I'd thought.

As the quiet between us grew, so did my anger. I could feel the ball of fire growing in my hand, running through my fingers as I wiggled them around.

"Don't make me do this," I said, hoping Drake's plan—whatever the fuck it was—was going to work. Merc did nothing, just sat down against the desk and stared.

"Blast him," Drake said, his voice cold and callous. Merc didn't budge. Not when I raised my hand to cast the fireball upon him. Not when I warned him I'd do it. I started to wonder if I was calling his bluff, or if he was calling mine. "Do it!" Drake shouted, and I did. I lobbed the blue fireball at Merc, who stood there and took it without resisting. It knocked him backward over the desk, and I scrambled over it to get to him, cursing at Drake along the way.

"What the fuck, Drake?"

"I proved my point."

"Which is what, exactly?" I asked, ripping Merc's shirt open to find seared flesh beneath. He was conscious and staring at me with curiosity.

"Jase... Dean? Is he talking to you about this?"

"Not a word," they replied in unison.

"My point," Drake said, drawing my attention back to him, "is that whatever bond he's severed doesn't matter. He's as inherently connected to you as the wolf is. That connection was never due to your bond. It was due to who you are and the fate that intertwined you."

"Because of his sacrifice for me before I was born..." Drake nodded. "And Knox's... the one he made to save my life." He nodded yet again.

I looked at Merc, who sat up, though it must have pained him to do so. I gave him a sheepish smile.

"I feel like 'sorry' might be a touch inadequate at the moment..."

"I will accept it anyway," he said, a dark smile tugging at his lips.

I muttered under my breath for my magic to heal him, and the wound on his chest quickly disappeared.

"Your bonding ritual was never the source of your connection," Drake said from the far side of the desk. "So mourning its loss is pointless."

"Time to suck it up and come home," Kat added with a wry smile.

Merc turned to Knox and stared for a moment, the two of them saying nothing.

"What say you, Trevor?" he asked, standing up to face his rival/ally/whatever those two were.

"I say it isn't my call to make. Piper is the one who needs what you can do. It's her decision."

Merc looked surprised by his response. "I thought you'd be more pleased to have me gone."

"Oh, don't get me wrong, I liked that part," Knox replied with a sober expression that slowly warmed the slightest bit, the familiar twinkle lighting his blue eyes. "But I like to win fair and square, not on a technicality."

The corner of Merc's mouth turned up. "Then consider the game afoot."

"No," Drake said, "no no no. No games. No contests. We've been over this. You three need to figure out how to coexist. End of story."

"Calm down, Drake," Knox groaned. "We're just fucking around. We got your memo loud and clear last time."

The warlock turned to Merc, who gave a small nod in agreement.

"Good."

"Let's get out of here," Kat said. "You guys can figure out the parameters of your dysfunctional relationship on the way. I can't wait to hear how this is going to play out." Judging by the amusement in her voice, she was finding it all very entertaining. Grizz's growl, however, told me he was far less enthused.

We all filed out of the former vampire king's mansion and made our way to the SUV. I stopped for a moment and looked back at it, thinking of everything it represented. All the bad memories I associated with it. Merc and Knox came to flank me as I stood and stared at it, my thoughts clearly readable in my expression.

"What do you think we should do with it?" Merc asked me, his tone sounding much more his own. He was back, hopefully for good.

"I hate this place," I said quietly.

"Then do what you do best, Piper," Knox said, looping his arm around my shoulders. I looked up at him to find mischief in his eyes.

"What's that?"

He smiled down at me. "Burn that fucker to the ground."

I turned to Merc, my eyes wide with surprise at what Knox had suggested.

My former mate simply nodded in agreement.

"Well you don't have to ask me twice," I said, thinking of all the former king had taken from me. How he'd manipulated me. Used me. Cast me aside when he thought I was of no use to him. Before I knew it, a blaze of fire shot out from my hands toward his home, igniting it in a second. It burned hot and fast, and within no more than five minutes, it had been reduced to ash. Just like the king himself.

The three of us turned our backs on that part of our lives and made our way to the vehicle. Together we'd change the course of the war and bring down the fey queen. Together we'd rewrite the rulebook, bringing about a new era for the supernatural world.

We'd do all that and more—*together.*

EPILOGUE

Knox came to me the next morning while I lay in bed, wanting a reprieve from chaos, if only for a few hours. He sat down on the edge of it, unable to meet my eyes, and took my hand in his. Whatever was wrong, I knew it couldn't be good.

"Tell me how you got out of there," he asked me, his voice deep and hollow. I sat up, moving closer to him, and told him what Liam had done. I left out the fey queen's involvement—that I now owed her a favor—and instead focused on how Liam had helped us escape the king. How, in the end, there had been a shred of the wolf Knox had once known still inside the killer he'd become. He turned to me with a pained expression and asked if I'd seen how he died. I hesitated, unsure how to answer his question. Eventually I told him what I knew—that he'd attacked the king and I hadn't seen him get up afterward. Then he pinned sharp eyes on me and asked if I thought he was dead.

I said yes.

He said *lie*.

He shot off the bed and paced the room like a man

possessed, rambling on about how we couldn't leave him there. That it would take a lot for the king to get rid of his weapon—that he'd likely punish him rather than dispose of him. That we couldn't abandon him to his fate again.

It wasn't long before I had a bedroom full of supernaturals, each looking to me for direction. Judging by the looks on their faces, whatever I decided would be good enough for them. I stood up slowly, petting Grizz as I walked past him to stand before Merc, who was at Knox's side. He nodded, and I took a deep breath, realizing what we had to do.

Return to motherfucking Faerie.

NEXT IN SERIES

BENEATH
THE
DUST

THE FORCE OF NATURE SERIES

AMBER LYNN
NATUSCH

ABOUT THE AUTHOR

Amber Lynn Natusch is the author of the bestselling *Caged*. She was born and raised in Winnipeg, and speaks sarcasm fluently because of her Canadian roots. She loves to dance and sing in her kitchen—much to the detriment of those near her—but spends most of her time running a practice with her husband, raising two small children, and attempting to write when she can lock herself in the bathroom for ten minutes of peace and quiet. She has many hidden talents, most of which should not be mentioned but include putting her foot in her mouth, acting inappropriately when nervous, swearing like a sailor when provoked, and not listening when she should. She's obsessed with home renovation shows, should never be caffeinated, and loves snow. Amber has a deep-seated fear of clowns and deep water...especially clowns swimming in deep water.